T0064511

A VOICE FROM THE RESTROOM

A VOICE FROM THE RESTROOM

CAREY WARD

authorHOUSE®

AuthorHouse™
1663 Liberty Drive
Bloomington, IN 47403
www.authorhouse.com
Phone: 1 (800) 839-8640

Published by AuthorHouse 07/27/2015

ISBN: 978-1-5049-2563-1 (sc)
ISBN: 978-1-5049-2562-4 (e)

Print information available on the last page.

Any people depicted in stock imagery provided by Thinkstock are models, and such images are being used for illustrative purposes only. Certain stock imagery © Thinkstock.

This book is printed on acid-free paper.

For Beth!

1

The plane dropped and Calvin's snack lurched up into his throat.

He was not sure if he should grab the bag in the pocket in front of him, or just hang on for dear life. He decided to hold on, praying his peanut butter cups would stay down. The plane quickly leaped forward, moving back into the line it had once been. Strangely enough, that forced Calvin's snack back down. His food was no longer in his throat, but was tossing and turning in his stomach. The diet Pepsi was not helping keep things calm.

Calvin had been late getting to the airport. Earlier in the day, his meeting had gone on longer than expected, forcing him to run through the parking lot to get to his car. The traffic had decided to hang around on the freeway into the late hours of the evening as if planning his delay. He hadn't had enough time to stop and eat, so he'd decided to pick something up at the airport.

He arrived at O'Hare with panic and hunger pains battling each other for supremacy. Looking at his watch, he had twenty minutes to get to his gate. Calvin raced to the baggage check, kicked off his shoes, threw his wallet, keys, cell phone, and watch into the little tub and jumped through the metal detector.

"Sir, could you step over here. We need to check your luggage."

He'd cringed; having your clothes displayed to the world was just one of the many fun attractions at the airport. Calvin was average for height and a little hefty for his size, if you call fifty pounds overweight hefty. Not he'd admit to that. His wife once asked him how he was doing on his diet. "Steady as ever, dear!" he'd replied. Of course it was steady: He had never started. And the resulting weight meant larger clothes and larger clothes were easier to see and much more fun for an audience to enjoy.

The luggage check resulted in Calvin's black boxers with yellow smiley faces getting spilled to the ground, and his acne cream falling on top. Funny how only the embarrassing things tend to fall. Calvin was forty-two years old and still had a small problem with acne; never major breakouts, but still troublesome when he was running meetings with important clients.

Calvin felt a small tug of relief with the luggage check complete. The TSA official dismissed him without a cavity check. Thank God for small favors. There was only ten minutes left until boarding, so Calvin did the only thing he could: He ran to the closest food outlet, a burger joint with freshly made, four-hour-old hamburgers sitting in a tanning bed. After ordering the double with bacon (it was all that was ready and the highest priced, of course), he skipped the fries and ordered a drink.

He was down to eight minutes when the cashier told him that the credit machine wasn't working, it was cash only. With only three dollars in his pocket, he sent the burger back to its suntan booth and Calvin was dismissed as if he had the plague. He found a newspaper stand still open and raced to it. Grabbing a bag of peanut butter cups and a diet Pepsi, he was off to his gate with five minutes to spare.

The one thing Calvin could count on was his plane being on time, even if he was not. He raced to the gate, stuffing his mouth with chocolate peanut buttery goodness that lodged in his throat. He chugged the diet Pepsi and the burp erupted in the face of the check-in assistant.

"Sorry about that," Calvin pretended as black-and-brown specks flew from his mouth. Fortunately, his Diet Pepsi had lime flavoring so the fruity smell overshadowed the peanut butter, he hoped. He was wrong.

Calvin entered the plane last. He walked through rows and rows of tired business travelers until he finally found his seat: the window seat of a three-seat aisle. After his fellow seatmates climbed out, and he could get to it, he practically fell into his seat.

He now took the chance to look over at his neighbors. There was a tall man in the aisle seat who felt he was more important than his seat allowed. He continued to look at his watch as if the plane would take that as a cue and begin to go.

The short woman next to him seemed to be close to Calvin's age. It was hard to tell, though, since she had the misfortune to have forgotten her adulthood: She was wearing an outfit that Calvin thought most teenage girls wouldn't dare wear. The outfit was tight, pushing her breasts up so far that other passengers might misinterpret them for floatation devices. It was okay, though: They made up for the roll of stomach hanging over her belt outlined from the tightness of the shirt. She finished off the ensemble with a skirt cut too short even for her height, which led to a tattoo on her ankle of a heart as she dared to be different, just like everybody else.

At this moment, Calvin realized he had to pee. As he began to get up, the light came on along with the voice of an woman who must have smoked a carton of cigarettes for breakfast.. The voice informed the travelers to stay in their seats until the plane had taken off and finished it's climb and leveled off. This didn't happen for another hour of squirming and discomfort for Calvin before the plane even took off on O'Hare's runway. A problem with an incoming flight had forced all traffic to stop where they were and not to move. The magic light above Calvin refused to stand down, which gave Calvin a bladder as tightly wound as his neighbor's shirt.

Upon the departure of the magic light and several thousand feet of airspace, Calvin was finally able to free himself, only to find that he was well back in a line of others with his problem. Apparently, the wait had had its effect on the entire flight. After waiting through at least three states from the rows of people to clear the heads, he was forced to squirm behind, Calvin was the second in line when smoky-voice came back on the line informing them that they were to return to their seats and that was that.

Apparently, the captain was going to take the plane around a storm that had surprised him, as it had stayed in place for two days without making any great moves. As they flew around the storm, the weather decided to take its cue and move for the first time in days and followed the plane. Hence the fall and leap with Calvin's dinner.

2

"Here it comes," Jerry whispered into his walkie-talkie. His tan jumpsuit claimed he was Sid. "Sid" was a baggage handler at the DFW airport. Sid's job, at least what he told the passengers, was to help poor travelers find their luggage whenever it suddenly got lost.

His real job was to find his mark and report via the walkie-talkie.

Sid, a studly-looking baggage-handler extraordinaire, was actually Jerry McNeill. He spent most of his mornings and afternoons at Computer City selling anything he could persuade a customer to buy. His main reason for working there was the 25% discounts on computer products and other electronics.

Jerry, rubbed the walkie-talkie just a little to feel it in his hand. This was a new brand and model of walkie-talkie, a Rino 220. With it, Jerry could talk to his partner, Ben, use GPS to see exactly where he was at all times, and get directions on where he was going. His favorite part, though, was the location beam. He could send his location to another person using a Rino 220, and vice versa. He had spotted it in Computer City's warehouse when he and Ben were unloading a shipment of Blue Ray's, external storage drives for computers and various audio equipment and knew instantly that he was going to get it.

"How long until they get here?" came over the sharp crack of the radio.

Jerry had the volume turned up too high and fidgeted with the knob until the sound was low enough not to broadcast around the room. "Ten minutes."

"Good. I'm having problems with this old microphone again. Seriously, it sucks. We got to get a new one."

Jerry used the walkie-talkie to see exactly where Ben was. The dot showed him to be in DFW airport, down the corridor and to the right from where Jerry was right now. He looked at the dot and thought about the last statement. The microphone they were using was a good one, but older than the walkie-talkies they were using. They had used it several times and tried to take good care of it. The problem was that they many times had to get into small places and climb through tightly constricted holes to do what they came to the airport to do. A suitcase would have been too obvious and in many cases too big, so they chose instead to use a backpack and look like college kids. The price of their lugging the equipment around in a canvas bag was the wear and tear on th equipment. The microphone was the first piece to go.

Again looking at the dot, mainly because he had nothing else to do other than wait, Jerry watched the dot that was Ben to see if it would move. Ben had not moved positions and Jerry knew Ben would not. He was set and they were ready. "Okay, it's good now," he said to Ben.

Jerry had met Benjamin Hawkins several years ago in school. They had had two things in common: They were bored in school and neither one was popular. They had met through a small circle of friends, and hit it off right away. Once Jerry realized how much Ben was into electronics, the friendship was cemented.

They referred to themselves as the real "Ben and Jerry." So, it wasn't original, but the jokes kept coming. They would constantly think of new ice cream flavors to define their latest pranks.

"Hey," the walkie-talkie cackled again.

"What?" Jerry whispered.

"I got it. Praline Prank."

"Naw, that's lame. How about Apricot Airport?"

"Apricot sucks."

"Whatever."

Silence came again as the plane rolled into view. The men on the ground were directing the plane into gate 22. That was when it donned on Jerry. "Hey, I got it," he nearly yelled in the walkie-talkie. "How about the Lord of Lemon Lime?"

For a second, Jerry did not think Ben had heard it. He was about to say it again when Ben replied.

"Seriously? Who is going to buy that? Forget it though, we have incoming."

"Perfect!"

3

The plane had been surrounded by a storm for nearly the entire flight, a storm that Calvin had yet to see out of the tiny window. Finally, this storm of the century relaxed its grip on the plane. Looking to see the little light go off and release its band of terror, Calvin was disappointed to see it stayed on. The smoky voice from the flight attendant got on the intercom and informed the passengers that they were entering the landing cycle and all trays should put in their upright position and everything put away, including electronics.

Calvin crossed his legs and turned his body slightly to the right in order to hold back the pressure building up. There was some pleasure to see that there were several others doing the same thing. *How do women hold it back* was his only thought.

The plane announced its arrival at Dallas Fort Worth with a thud on the runway. The landing added greatly to the pressure building within Calvin and the others' bladders. Fortunately, the plane rolled directly to its cocoon walkway.

The stampede that ensued was limited in its assault on the gate entrance due to the miniature aisle that the passengers tried to move down. The stop and go of the aisle traffic was a constant reminder to Calvin that his trip had yet to complete its mockery of him. Only when he reached the doorway and felt the still, stale air of airport hallways did he feel relieved.

"We hope you enjoyed your flight," the flight attendant grumbled..

The flight attendant was a very short middle-aged blonde whose hair could be plastic as it curved out and away from her neck. The high curve in front reminded him of the Big Hair of the eighties. As Calvin looked to comment, he realized that she was not looking at the passengers at all, rather sending them verbally on their way. He was half expecting her to start saying "Bye,-bye" in the classic *Saturday Night Live* skit, but was pushed from behind by one of his fellow cows trying to stampede out.

Finally in the airport hallway, Calvin spotted the restroom. He did not pass Go, nor did he take any detours. Heading directly for Start, he felt the buildup begin. Several passengers were passing him up as they sprinted for their luggage. The only thing between him and his goal was an airport serviceman [which is what, exactly?]. The excitement rose in his loins, freedom was only steps away when it happened.

"Excuse me, sir," the serviceman said.

"Yes?" Calvin asked trying not to be rude while simultaneously trying not to openly display himself doing the pee-pee dance.

"We seem to have had a mix up with some of the bags. You just came from O'Hare Airport, correct?"

"Yes. What happened with the luggage?" Calvin asked, adding another notch to the Trip of the Century.

"Oh, some of it got onto the wrong belt."

That was the fastest screwing-up Calvin had ever heard about, even for an airport, but he kept his thoughts to himself for two reasons: The less talking that went on, the quicker he could get to the restroom, and two, they still had his luggage and he did not want it to take another unexpected detour because of his smart mouth.

"I just need your name and I will get your luggage on the right belt."

"Calvin. Calvin James." It did not dawn on him that the baggage handler was only talking to him, or that the other passengers were moving past him to the baggage claim area. It only mattered that this nice young man was helping him out and that he was standing in his way to relief.

"Thank you sir, I will take care of everything."

"No problem," Calvin replied as another passenger moved in to talk to the serviceman.

"Is something wrong?" was all he heard the passenger asking the attendant as Calvin made his dash for the stall of freedom.

4

The others had all left or were finishing up as Calvin entered the restroom. He quickly found an open urinal and felt ten pounds erupt from him. It seemed hours flew by before he was done. The passengers that came before him were all done and washing their hands and exiting the restroom except for one man who hurried out of the bathroom straight from the one of the stalls. *Mental note*, Calvin thought, *no shaking hands with that guy*.

Finally, Calvin moved to the sink to wash his hands. Standing in the mirror was an old, tired fellow with bags forming under his eyes. *Man*, Calvin thought, *I'm getting old*.

"CALVIN," a voice said with a boom.

Calvin jerked his hands up and water sprayed out of the sink onto the floor. He looked around to see someone speak to him, but nobody was there.

"CALVIN," the voice bellowed again.

This time Calvin looked for a speaker. He was half expecting to hear someone tell him his luggage was on its way to Germany.

"CALVIN, THIS IS GOD."

No movement, no breath, nothing. Calvin didn't move a muscle, not an inch. It took nearly an eternity before he took a breath, and it was deep and hard.

"CALVIN JAMES. YOU HAVE BEEN NEGLECTING ME, HAVEN'T YOU?"

Calvin thought hard for a second: *No, this is not happening. Someone is playing a trick on me.* He looked around again, but nobody was there.

"NO NEED TO LOOK FOR ME, CALVIN; YOU KNOW WHERE I AM."

Calvin wanted to run out of the restroom as fast as possible, but something kept him in there. Something wanted him to hear.

"CALVIN JAMES. I NEED YOU."

No. This has to be a joke. This is not happening. Not again. Calvin James the man who heard God. Calvin James the man who went crazy.

"CALVIN, SAVE MY PEOPLE, CALVIN. SAVE MY PEOPLE."

Then there was nothing. For a moment there was only the drip of the faucet and silence. Suddenly a man turned the corner and startled Calvin.

"Did you hear that?" Calvin asked, hoping the man would say yes and his fears would be at ease. But he didn't. Calvin was the only one to hear.

Calvin, he asked himself, *was that God*?

Then in a run that would put Olympic athletes to shame, Calvin raced for the door and was gone.

5

They had had to wait over five minutes for the last person to leave the restroom. When they were finally alone, Ben handed the equipment down to Jerry, who'd come from his post, and then climbed down out of the vent located at the back of the restroom. They shoved the equipment into the backpack. Then Jerry took off his top layer to reveal normal student-looking clothes. He stuffed the uniform on top of the equipment and then hoisted the backpack over his shoulder, put a worn-out John Deere hat on his head, and walked with Ben out of the restroom, all the while trying hard not to break down in laughter.

The two forced the tears back as they passed the first luggage claim area and walked down the hallway almost until it ended. Here, they exited out of the airport and went directly to the parking lot. It was at this point that the tears would no longer hold back.

"He took off, dude," Jerry began. "It was priceless."

"Seriously," Ben added in between fits of giggles. "I didn't think it would work. That microphone kept going out. We really need a new one."

Jerry ignored the last statement. Instead, the picture of the middle aged man hysterically running out of the men's bathroom kept replaying in his mind.

"What was up with that 'save my people' crap?" Jerry asked.

"I didn't have enough time. That other guy walked in before I could really get going. It was all I could think of to say."

"But, 'save my people'? He must have serious issues to fall for that one."

"I know. I was having a Moses moment. Remember that Richard Burton movie when he played Moses? It just kept coming back to my mind as I was talking to that guy."

"You mean the Ten Commandments? That wasn't Richard Burton, it was that guy from the Rifleman."

"What? No way. That guy is way gone."

"Whatever. Still, it was priceless."

The two climbed into Ben's rusted-out yellow 1979 VW bug and drove off.

6

Calvin sat in his company-paid, two-year-old gold Toyota Camry down in the parking garage. His knuckles were white from the death grip he had on the steering wheel. His forehead had a mark across it from his banging it on the steering wheel. This was not the day to be a steering wheel for Calvin James.

Sweat trickled down his face and dripped onto his pants. Calvin, in his own terms, was freaking out. What had just happened? Was it real or did he imagine it? Somebody had to be playing a trick on him. Calvin was waiting any moment for someone to jump out with a video camera and surprise him as they laughed in his face and said "Gotcha!"

He looked around the garage; there was nobody there. There was nobody trying to surprise him. There were only five cars in all near him, and they held no television production company. He was alone.

"This can't be happening. Not to me. No." The thoughts slipped from his mouth as if he were trying to talk himself out of believing what had just happened. It was not working.

He continued banging his head and slapping the steering wheel until he heard the sound of a car. It shook him out of his stupor and made him react. He started his car and drove out of the parking spot and down the first ramp in the garage. Maybe it was a van. It had to be. Someone had filmed it all and was trying to get away.

Calvin roared the car down the aisle, heading for the final ramp that would take him to the bottom level and eventual out of the parking garage. He took the ramp too fast, skidding slightly, but he steered into the skid and was fine. He roared down the ramp and suddenly slammed on his brakes, squealing the tires on the asphalt. A beat-up yellow VW bug was crossing and Calvin nearly ran into him. Two young boys were in it, eyes round in shock and mouths set in fear as Calvin nearly collide with them. They look like they'd been crying, although he could barely see the one in the passenger seat. The two said something to each other, which Calvin couldn't hear, and they gassed their car and drove off. Calvin just sat there for a moment.

Way to go big, man. You just scared the crap out of two kids.

Once the rusted old car had moved on, Calvin drove a little more carefully around the parking garage. There was only one van on the entire level. A red minivan with a coat hanger used for an antenna. Calvin got out and looked in it. There was nothing.

Calvin drove around the garage for a while longer. When no vans showed up with television lights, he knew there was no other place to look. He sat in his car with the brakes on in front of the exit, just staring out. His thoughts failed him, his mind a blank.

A horn bellowed behind him. Calvin jumped in his seat. He took a quick glance in the rearview mirror partly in excitement, but it was only a woman in a BMW wanting to exit. Then, with a heavy sigh, Calvin moved the car into the last parking space before the exit and turned the car off. He watched as the woman pulled past him and then closed his eyes and leaned back in the seat.

The memory played out in front of him as if it had just happened. Martin had been one of his best friends in the entire world. He'd loved Martin like a brother. The two of them had played together for so many years; he could not remember when they hadn't. Their days together would last so long they blurred together. Sometimes they'd play basketball, or ride bikes. Most of the time, they played on the railroad tracks. Well, not directly on them, but around them.

Martin lived on the other side of the tracks, literally, in identical subdivisions. Each of their houses was almost in the middle of their street, so they only had two ways of getting to each other's house. One way was to walk to the end of the street, walk across the railroad tracks by walking down the main thoroughfare, and then walk down the other person's street. The easier and highly preferred method was to jump the tiny chain-link fence, run down the slope that led to the railroad tracks, cross the tracks, run up the other slope, and climb up and over the chain-link fence on the other side. The latter was about ten minutes shorter and loads more fun. It won out.

They never really played directly on the tracks except for trying to balance on the beams or putting pennies on the tracks to see if they would flatten out. Rarely did they find those pennies. When they did, they were so beaten up that Calvin couldn't tell if was their original, or somebody else's.

It was after a long game of horse that the two realized how utterly bored they were. Spring breaks were nice, but dragged on when all of your friends were out of town. It was just the two of them. Calvin's memory blurred as to why they'd gone down the slope that day. He assumed, now, that there'd been nothing else to do and the two of them liked playing there.

The memory came rushing back, though, when he remembered the sound of the horn. They'd been playing on the tracks, trying to dig underneath one of the beams. They had finally gotten to the point that they could each put an arm down and touch fingers underneath. It was that exact moment that the horn sounded.

Calvin looked back at the sound and tried to stand up; his arm got caught, but he was able to pull it free. He stood up and turned to face the oncoming train. It was turning around a grove of trees and was getting close to the intersection. He moved off to the side as quickly as he could and began to climb the slope when he realized Martin was not with him.

Calvin turned back, expecting to see Martin climbing the other slope toward his own home—they were going to have to wait for the train to pass before figuring out what to do. But the slope was empty. Calvin looked down and his heart stopped. Martin was still kneeling down on the tracks.

"Hurry up, there's a train coming!" he yelled as if Martin had suddenly gone deaf.

"I can't, it's stuck!"

Just the thought of the words, even now, made Calvin's heart accelerate.

The memory became horridly vivid as Calvin remembered the sound of the train pounding toward Martin. Martin, now in a panic, was pulling frantically at his arm, trying to break free. The horn blew as if hoping its mere sound could free the boy from his perch. Then it came.

"SAVE HIM." The words were spoken as if someone were standing next to him. Calvin looked around, but there was nobody there, and yet the voice continued.

"SAVE HIM."

Calvin looked to the train and then to Martin. His heart was now beating so fast that he thought it might explode. He wanted with every beat of his heart to race to Martin to save him, to pull him from that hole and drag him off those tracks. It was his feet that refused to budge. Finally, after seemingly an eternity, he began to move. It was too late, the train crossed the thoroughfare and came barreling fast toward Martin. Calvin took one-step toward him, then seeing Martin's helpless face, he looked away.

The train raced by with a screech that pierced his ears. Calvin could not look at the tracks, but kept his face hidden, tears flowing from his cheeks. It felt as if the train would never stop, even though its wheels were no longer moving. Finally, after the longest skid Calvin had ever heard, the train came to a stop. Neighbors from both sides were coming out to see what had happened. The sound of a passing train was normal; the sound of one screeching to a stop was not.

Calvin thought he had failed God. It had to be his voice, and yet Calvin hadn't listened. Every fiber in his being had begun to shred as Calvin fell to his knees. What was worse, failing God, or failing your friend? Calvin had failed both and he knew it. His mom had raced from the house and found Calvin on his knees and lifted him up. It was not her asking him what was wrong that woke him up, it was her next statement.

"Why is Martin getting yelled at?" she asked. "Did you to do something?"

Calvin looked up and over at the train. Peeking between the two cars directly in front of him was an opening. That opening showed a very alive and scared Martin being read the riot act by his mom. The visual soothed Calvin's sorrow, but not his guilt. He had still failed.

It was not until Martin's house had been sold the next month that the two spoke. Apparently, Martin's mom had had enough of the tracks and was ready to move away. Calvin asked what had happened, how he had gotten free.

"It felt like somebody pulled me up and freed me from the tracks. I didn't do anything. I looked around, but nobody was there."

The two said their goodbyes that were so distant that forgiveness was not even a thought. They merely waved to each other and walked off.

Calvin released his grip on the steering wheel. His knuckles were white and almost felt stuck in that position. The voice played in his mind as it had almost every day of his life. It wasn't until he got married that the voice had quieted down. Then he had had kids and the voice seemed to disappear. Now, in an airport bathroom, a voice comes back to say save his people.

He knew it was probably a joke. Anybody could say it to anybody and get a good kick out of watching. However, there had not been anyone around and the Voice knew his name. Calvin shook it off. It could not be. This could not be a second chance. Then, with a deep breath, Calvin started his car and reversed out of the parking spot.

"No, it had to be a joke," he whispered to himself, and then he put the car in drive and pulled away. In the back of his mind, Calvin was hoping that he was driving away from the voice as well.

7

The sun greeted Janiyah in a warm welcome that shined across her face. She had been allowed to get outside during her time here, but this was different. This was freedom. Sure, she had been able to go home at night and spend some of the weekends at home, too, but the days had been spent at the hospital.

Janiyah looked up into the sky and closed her eyes to allow the sun to fully engulf her face. It felt good. Her doctor had said that she no longer needed full-time treatment; she was ready for in-home "therapy." Janiyah knew he meant that they were just keeping an eye on her, but it did not matter. She was allowed to go back to school, see her friends, and resume her life.

For the past six months, Janiyah had been kept at the TimberPoint Mental Health Hospice. She'd been reduced to tears several times, but had kept to her story. She had heard the voice of God. It was almost a month ago when she realized the voice was not coming to her anymore. She gave up. She had confessed to believing it was all in her head. This wasn't necessarily the truth that she felt, but it pushed her closer to the freedom she craved.

Finally, the drugs stopped coming, allowing her to be more alert. She followed this with no fits, no fighting about the voice. It now did not exist. Janiyah had been told so many times by her doctors that the voices were not real, just made up illusions in her mind, that even she'd started to question herself. Then after several weeks of proper behavior and answering the questions the way she knew the doctors were pushing her to answer, she was set free to resume her life.

Janiyah's shoulder got squished as her mom reached around her back with one arm and squeezed Janiyah into her side. Another full hug from dad that lifted her off the ground, and then she was escorted to the car. David, her dad, got into his seat first, ready to drive away from this place as fast as his foot and the Chrysler 300 would let him. Aleesha waited for her daughter to get in first before sitting down.

Janiyah hesitated after she opened the backseat car door and turned to look at the hospital. Her face gave nothing away, but the look in her eyes would have sent her doctor into such a panic, the entire staff would be called in to haul her back.

"I know I heard that voice," she said quietly to herself. And with a self satisfied smile, she turned back to the car and sat down.

Aleesha watched with happiness as her baby climbed into the car, not hearing Janiyah speak. It had been hard for Janiyah, but it had been hard for her and David, too. The whispers and stares were nothing compared to the hopeless feeling they had shared in not being able to help their daughter. *She has overcome a lot*, Aleesha thought, *we all have*. Then she sat down in the front seat with a sigh and a belief that it was all finally behind them.

David spun the car out before her door was properly closed, which slammed it shut and he sped out of the parking lot, leaving the hospital and painful memories behind them.

8

The train horn woke Calvin early the next morning. He looked for where it was coming from, and only found the alarm clock buzzing. The dream had been so vivid, Calvin felt as if he were living the entire scene over again. There was just one part that did not fit: *His* voice kept repeating over and over "there are no second chances."

He had chosen not to tell his wife Becca about the restroom incident. She was already asleep when he'd gotten home and he hadn't wanted to wake her. Now, he just could not get it out of his head that it was a joke that he'd taken way too seriously. Instead, Calvin decided to ignore the event and focus on getting to the office on time.

Breakfast was the usual cheerios and orange juice with random fruit that Becca had cut the night before. As he sat down at the table, Calvin unfolded the morning paper in preparation for a relaxing morning that would never come. It never did.

"Mom, can I have my breakfast now?" Adam asked.

It appeared that the boy had just woken up, but Calvin knew better. Adam didn't believe in brushing his hair. Every morning Adam would wake up with half of his head flattened down while the other pointed and curved in so many different directions that even the best hair stylist would be at a loss to achieve that kind of perfection. Calvin and Becca tried to tame the wild beast, but always failed. Several times Becca would even wet it down and put gel in it just to get it to settle down. Ten seconds after she was done, Adam would just shake his head and "poof" the magic hair would return. Eventually they gave up. They secretly assumed the hair was a conspiracy against parenting, a conspiracy they would keep an eye on.

"Uggh, can't you flush the toilet?" Maureen exclaimed as she thumped Adam on the side of the head.

"Don't," Adam replied. Mr. Comeback.

Maureen was about to be out of single digits soon as her birthday loomed. Just like most girls her age, she was already hitting the teenage years running full speed. Skirts were getting just a little shorter, as the attitude tended to increase just a little bit. As Maureen wanted more and more privacy, the bathroom she and Adam shared seemed to get smaller and smaller. This created much of the tension that always came crashing down to the family table.

"Stop it, you two," was Becca's usual response. She used it each day; it clearly had the reverse effect.

The standard dramatic performance for school mornings was well rehearsed in the James household.

Act 1: Son shows up asking for breakfast that was being made. Act 2: Sister comes down, thumps brother, and creates fuss. Act 3: Mom then attempts a truce as dad sits at breakfast table, trying to ignore anything that might cause him to move off his schedule, which he never achieved anyway.

"Calvin, can you do something about this?" Becca demanded.

"Stop it, you two." Mr. Comeback, Sr.

"Dad, can you tell Troll Doll over here that he needs to flush? It's disgusting."

"Adam, you need to flush; we've talked about that."

"Okay," Adam reluctantly agreed. Then, to show he was actually paying no attention at all, he asks, "Dad, what's a Troll Doll?"

"I finished my book last night. You would like it," Becca said causing Calvin to cringe on a bite of cheerios.

For the last three years Becca had been reading self help books. Some of the books dealt with business, some with personality, and others with nutrition and health. Lately, it had been business. Of course, every book she read was dead on correct.

"Absolutely, this is it," was the statement that came from the finality of each word-processed. It mattered little whether it conflicted with the previous absolute word of the previous book. All that mattered was that she had read it and it had pulled on her emotions enough to get her excited. She now knew exactly how to get rich through marketing, real estate, working from home, and every pyramid scheme known to mankind. The problem was the next book would be out to say that those were not the ways, only this was the direct approach, and Becca would follow. At least she would follow all the way up to the end of the book, then commence to act on ignoring her own advice and search the internet for something else she was missing.

It had taken Calvin a while to figure this out. He, being a slow learner of women, had at first tried to argue his point, clearly identifying the gaps in the thinking and the fact they had little capital from which to begin. It finally dawned on him one day to let Becca have her way, as she would anyway through repetitive efforts that could force any terrorist to surrender.

"Okay dear, just put it by my nightstand." The nightstand was that of a black hole of self-help books. Many have entered, none have returned.

It was with great joy that Calvin finished his bowl of regularity and removed himself from the table. Becca was still speaking to him of the importance of the latest book, "Rich man, poor efforts" as the water faucet drowned out her reasoning.. Finally, his "yes dear" was out of the way and Calvin could return to this already disrupted schedule and head for work. A plan that he would regret following.

9

The drive down the George Bush Freeway was as pleasant as possible. It was still remarkable to Calvin that more people didn't realize how fast it was. He had purchased a toll pass that glued to his windshield just behind the rearview mirror. This allowed him easy access to pass through the gates without slowing down. Considering that he had to pass three gates on his way to work, it saved him quite a bit of time.

Usually, Calvin had ESPN blaring on the radio. The NFL draft was quickly approaching, and the Cowboys had been so bad for so long, he figured at least once they would get it right on draft day. He was hoping to hear some good news. Maybe they actually had a plan to draft someone who could have an impact for their defensive line, but Calvin wasn't holding his breath.

Today was different. Instead of blaring the radio, Calvin drove in silence. He had thoughts on his mind. As he sped down the tollway, passing the first gate, a van that had taken the time to pay its toll with cash began to exit the gate and reenter the freeway when it was forced to swerve into incoming traffic and cut off Calvin's route, forcing Calvin to cut into the left lane. Horns blared all around as Calvin was ready to tell the driver that his mother had actually been a dog and he was her son, when he read the side of the van.

Second Chance Repair. WE FIX WHAT YOU HAVE UNDONE.

Calvin stared at the van for a second when another melody of orchestrated car horns disrupted him from his thoughts. With a humph, he was off again, passing the van and pulling into the right lane, allowing the NASCAR wannabes to pull ahead. Several gave him the one-finger salute. Calvin waved to each one and smiled.

This was going to be a long day.

Calvin turned off at the Central Expressway and went south. His exit was only a few exits away. Pulling off the highway, Calvin passed familiar sights. First, there was the 5,000th car dealership in the area, then a massive church, and then a strip center in which half of the tenants had been there for over two decades and the other tenants had left and not been replaced. The tenants that currently remained had not changed their signs since the late 'eighties. Weather and poor upkeep had kept them from retaining their glory, if they'd ever actually had any.

As Calvin drove past the dealership, he looked over to see a giant inflatable wheel that stretched upwards almost two stories standing on the roof, which stood over another sign that said CLOSEOUT SALE. The dealership had been displaying this sign for nearly two years. It was a wonder that they had a parking lot full of cars.

Calvin then passed the church. It had been built later than the other buildings so it stood out, as it was clean, well kept, and did not have a giant blue gorilla standing on top of it. Each time Calvin passed the church, he read the giant sign that stood out next to the frontage road. The sign was a digital display that probably cost the congregation a few months' of their paychecks, but easily stood out in this neighborhood. It usually read in lighted lettering what the pastor was preaching on each given week. Calvin drove by and had to do a double take and look back at the sign as he passed it. This time the sign read, "Faster than a locomotion, yeah, you know who." This time there was no humph from Calvin.

There was only the silence of the car with the hum of the engine in the background.

10

Ben waited in the warehouse docking area. They had pulled this off before, but security at the store had gotten tight. People had been stealing from the store since it was created, and always would, but up to this point, management had thought it was an outside job. The inside jobs had gone on unnoticed, that is, until recently.

Ben had been working at Best Electronics for almost two years now. Jerry came on board on his recommendation. They had been playing around with pranks before, mostly phone calls, when they suddenly had a brilliant idea and they "borrowed" some equipment from the store and used it to play their first big prank. They hid a speaker in the bushes of their school. When somebody walked by, they either spoke to that person or made some rude noise and they filmed the entire thing.

Being put in in-school suspension for almost a month was worth it.

After several months of making small-scale pranks on neighbors, schoolmates, and local citizens, Ben and Jerry realized something: They were bored. There was more out there and they needed to find it. The "borrowing" grew, as the two needed more and more equipment to reach their goals. Eventually, Jerry said what they were doing was outright stealing. The two looked at each other and shrugged their shoulders. Both were okay with it. Stealing was bad only if you got caught. Besides, they needed the stuff. They approved their decision by telling themselves that it was not hurting anybody. The only thing that would even partially be hurt was a big business that overworked and underpaid its employees. Ben and Jerry decided they were fine with this and Best Electronics could deal with it.

They began to stockpile their loot by storing it in the warehouse. One of them would take the item to the back, stating to fellow workers that it was the wrong item, and the other one would take it and hide it as the first person returned to the store with the correct item. Since both of them worked the closing shift, it was not uncommon for them to be found straightening up the warehouse. It was pretty easy, actually. They just took the item and tossed it out behind one of the dumpsters as they were taking out the trash. Then they would pick it up late at night after everyone had gone home. The missing items would be assumed to have been stolen by either a customer, miscounted, or somewhere else in the store. It didn't hurt that both Ben and Jerry were on the inventory team and could manipulate the totals any time they needed to.

Then, one day, there was a meeting with the managers. Both Ben and Jerry had stayed away from any kind of promotion, so they were not invited. Promotion meant that the two could not be on closing duty together. It also meant more responsibility, which neither of them wanted.

Lance Albright, their immediate supervisor, who thought there was no way his boys would be the problem, leaked the manager's meeting to them. Apparently, the brass was getting smarter and beginning to look at the staff for possible thefts.

The lock down had been going on for almost a month when Ben and Jerry realized that they had to figure out a new plan; the lock down wasn't going to change soon. Their duties had been rearranged so Ben and Jerry were not on closing duty together. In addition, new security details had kept them from bringing any equipment back to the warehouse without supervisor approval.

Jerry walked through the doors that led to the showroom. His face told it all.

"Sorry, but I can't do it. They're watching too close."

"I know. This blows. We need a new microphone. Any chance you can mark it defective without anyone knowing?"

"No. Lance has to approve it and test it personally."

"Seriously, we've got to figure this out. That microphone is messed up."

"I know."

The two were silent, looking around the warehouse as if an answer would appear in the form of a neon sign, or a giant foam finger pointing at one of them, screaming, "I got it, I got it!" None came.

Ben looked at Jerry with the news that he had been holding back, having hoped the microphone would be his way in. "Hey, remember that girl that got us busted a couple of years ago?"

"You mean the one that went crazy? Dude, that was awesome. Too bad we couldn't tell anybody about it— that would have been an all-time classic on the 'Net."

"Yeah, well. There is a chance we can up the stakes."

"What do you mean?" Jerry asked.

"She just got released back to school with a clean bill of health."

Jerry looked around the warehouse harder now. After still not being able to find his sign, he looked back at Ben. "Okay. First we need a new microphone, and then we get the girl."

11

Breakfast was more of a forced march than a pleasant experience. Janiyah's stomach was churning so fast she thought that at any moment she might spew the pancakes all over the table. Instead of actually putting in a mouthful and chewing, she felt it better to nibble at one pancake and swallow quickly. Each bite was chased by a gulp of orange juice, a deep breath, and a tiny prayer.

The rest of the morning was more of the same. Brushing her teeth was a chore and picking out the best outfit was impossible. Janiyah finally settled on a faded pair of blue jeans with a hole in the left knee. The pink socks and pink tennis shoes that accompanied those matched a pink t-shirt that said "Princess" in sequins on the chest. She didn't have a matching purse so she chose a white one to go with it.

Finally, Janiyah grabbed her backpack and headed downstairs for the front door. Her mom and dad were standing there waiting for her.

"I can still drive you, if you want. There's plenty of time." David almost pleaded with her.

"It's only a few blocks, Dad." She knew how important today was for them, too. But this she had to do herself.

Aleesha reached her first and wrapped Janiyah up in the biggest bear hug. Even if she wanted to escape, the hug was too all-consuming to allow her to break free. It was okay; Janiyah enjoyed it. She loved her parents and was glad they were there for this moment, too. Her mom let go with a smile and stepped back. Then her dad bent over and hugged Janiyah as well, whispering into her ear how proud he was of her. Then she was out the door, down the front walk, and on her way to school.

Her best friend, Jessica, was already at school. She was probably preparing for the academic decathlon competition that was coming up. Both Jessica and Janiyah had qualified for the team as they'd prepared to start high school, before the voices had started speaking, and before she'd been sent to the hospice. Now she didn't know if she'd be allowed on the team.

The tougher, more immediate issue with Janiyah, though, was that she was now walking to school all alone.

Growing up in a mostly white neighborhood was not all that bad. It was quieter than where they'd lived before, and it was much safer. The problem was fitting in. Most of the parents were nice. They would smile when they told her that so and so was not home or busy doing homework. Somehow, little so-and-so was always doing homework or never at home.

That was what made Jessica so great. She saw Janiyah for the person she was, a good girl and a better friend. The first time they'd met, it almost fell apart, but turned into a friendship that they believed would always last. As Janiyah approached the final intersection that stood before the school, she concentrated on remembering the first time they'd met. It always put her in a better mood.

Janiyah had been riding her bike down the street, alone, paying no attention to anything around her, just enjoying the sun on her face. As she was rounding the corner onto her street, she could see two boys kitty-corner to her, point and stare. She'd already felt the isolation on her street, but the staring and whispering had increased. She'd tried talking to her mom, but was met with "try to work it out, give it time," answer. Janiyah peddled faster to try to escape the torment of the boys' stares.

As she rode closer to her house, Janiyah spotted two girls on their driveway, jumping rope. One was a little older and was watching over the younger girl. The older girl looked close to Janiyah's age, maybe a year older; the younger girl was much younger. As Janiyah rode closer, the older girl spoke.

"Wow, looking at you, I bet you can jump really well."

Everything upon moving to this new house boiled up in Janiyah at once and erupted in such a manner that it surprised Janiyah as much as the other girls.

"What do you mean, 'looking at me'? I am no different than any of you. I wish people would get it out of their head that I am different. Just 'cause I'm black, doesn't mean I'm different. It doesn't mean I'm a great athlete 'cause I'm black. Maybe I'm smart, too, you ever think of that?" She glared at the older girl then, just to prove her point, glared at the little girl.

The older girl looked red in the face and tried clearing her throat. She said something that was unintelligible, so Janiyah looked at her again.

"What did you say?"

"I was only talking about your shoes. They are those air shoes by that basketball player. Aren't they good for jumping?"

Janiyah could have crawled under a rock and hidden right then and there. She had finally confronted someone in this neighborhood about their bigotry, only to find that the girl was not talking about skin color, but about shoe styles. Janiyah hadn't known what to say. She looked from the big girl to the little girl, who was about to cry, and then back to the big girl. Then, without knowing what else to say, she simply apologized and turned to walk away.

"Wait," the big girl said as she ran to Janiyah. "Do you want to jump rope with us?"

And it was really as simple as that. A few minutes jumping rope, a few jokes about the shoes and the moment had passed and the two girls were already friends. Even Jessica's little sister, Heather, was beginning to enjoy the new member of their circle.

Later that day, Jessica and Janiyah went inside to grab a snack of lemonade and Rice Krispie treats. They laughed so hard at how they met; lemonade came out of Janiyah's nose.

Someone snickering interrupted Janiyah's thoughts. She looked around to see several other kids walking past her to cross the street.

"God must have told her to stay there and laugh," one of the boys said, thinking he was out of distance.

Janiyah lost her smile and, with a heavy sigh, began to walk across the street toward school.

It was going to be a long day.

12

Calvin parked his car and took a moment to put what he had heard the previous day into perspective: It was not as if he were hard-headed, just reluctant to believe that this was circling around him. The signs could have been there for their own reasons, and coincidences are more common than signs. Therefore, Calvin felt comfortable forgetting about it and tempting fate. He got out of his car thinking "Prove it" but refused to admit to whom he was talking. That would've been going a little too far.

Three steps toward the parking lot elevator, Calvin stepped on a can of Yoo-Hoo and nearly broke his ankle trying to right himself. As he did so, he almost cussed out the Individual he was trying very hard to hide from. He meekly looked up into the ceiling of the parking structure and quietly said he was sorry.

The morning flew by with meetings and handling his clients. Calvin hadn't spent much time feeding his children when they were infants, nor did he spend much time around infants now. Nevertheless, he knew infant formula and this now consumed his life. Scottish Rite Hospital in Dallas called him for a problem in their latest shipment, but they still loved the product. They needed more lactic-free formula, which Calvin had put in for this order. His problem had always been the warehouse.

Angela's Baby Food was the third best-selling baby formula in the Southwest and was moving into the other states. Their motto was that Babies Come First, which of course meant after they were paid for their extensive research, marketing, long dinners, and multiple nightclub visits spent in search of clients.

Calvin was the top sales manager in the Southwest and had recently been asked to start handling the North sales in order to grow the company nationally. Gary now handled West Coast sales and Karli handled the East while all three continued to split portions of the South. Each manager had three sales representatives underneath him or her. Calvin and the other managers each reported to Candace.

Candace was one of those women who were not outright beautiful, but are very hard to look away from. She'd worked her way through college by stripping. She'd become so involved with the lifestyle that she'd begun to attend private parties of the upper-class clients. She'd worked late during one party as the party wound its way into the early morning. Exhausted and a little drunk, Candace began to lose track of time and her senses. Eventually, she passed out and woke up unknowingly pregnant. Nine months later, she was a single mother on a crusade to change her life. Her choice was to begin selling infant formula and destroying men by any means necessary. She became successful at both.

Typically, when both Gary and Calvin were in town at the same time and not on sales trips, they'd go to lunch together.

Sometimes Karli would go, but she preferred to eat at her desk and work. Karli was a working mom and the primary parent. She typically had to skip meals in order to keep her production levels up. Angela's was not known for job completion, rather just busywork. The more active you appeared, the better you were treated, regardless of what came from it. Currently, Karli was working on a list of possible retail chains that would benefit from baby formula, all of which she would never visit. The list alone would buy her two days of Candace-free time.

Calvin had been thinking about A Heroes Hero sub sandwich shop. The old-fashioned sub sandwich place was one of Gary and Calvin's favorite spots. They visited the place so often that the owners would see them get out of their car and wave. If Calvin and Gary waved back and sat down in the outside picnic benches, Johnny the owner would immediately prepare them their usual.

Just the thought of sitting outside on a sunny, 78-degree day, enjoying a hero with ham and pepperoni and plenty of salt made the day possible. Other places were scared to put on salt, but not Hero's. Calvin wasn't sure, but he thought that Hero's might even have a salt lick set up in the back.

Only today, Calvin did not get the chance to enjoy the sloppy goodness wrapped up in a sourdough bun. Today, Calvin's lunchtime was spent with Candace, a sloppy taste of evil wrapped up in a ball-busting fist of angst. It was exactly three minutes before Calvin stepped out the door. He had actually stopped working fifteen minutes before, and was currently pretending to be analyzing a spreadsheet of competitor's quarterly sales numbers when she walked in to let him know his presence was required. No heroes for Calvin.

Today's subject was Calvin's mid-state sales rep's lack of experience. Pete had been hired by Candace against Calvin's better judgment. Her rational was that Calvin could mentor the young rep. Calvin thought it was a way for Candace to keep him busier than he already was. If so, it was working very well.

Pete had been a customer service rep for Angela's before moving up. He'd had no experience and offered little in promise other than that he was very hyper, but good-looking and male, all of which offered Candace plenty of reason to despise him, which meant she wanted him closer to her. The closer anyone got to Candace in the business, the more control she had over them. Calvin often wondered how Karli had been able to move up so effectively, considering she was not a man and had no balls to bust.

It took almost the entire lunch hour for Calvin to convince Candace that Pete's sales numbers looked like they did because he was just getting started, even though he'd been on the job for nearly six months. The fact that Pete wasn't qualified and Candace hired him despite Calvin's protest was never brought up. Calvin liked his manhood and preferred keeping it. Candace finally agreed to Calvin's defense and temporarily pardoned Pete. Calvin was set loose with a scowl and a warning to get the numbers up. Being set loose from Candace's office was like escaping the electric chair. It was just a pardon until you were put back on line for another chance. Calvin loved his job.

Stomach growling and manhood still intact, Calvin decided to find a quick bite to eat. The diner in the bottom floor of the eight-story office complex was closed today due to a salmonella scare dealing with lettuce, spinach, or some kind of green leafy thing that shouldn't be eaten for lunch anyway. Calvin decided to find the closest Burger Barn and take his chance with a quarter pound of fat and starch instead.

There wasn't enough time for Calvin to get out, so he went through the drive-thru and asked for a Number One meal that included fries and a Diet Coke, which was necessary to balance out the starch, salt, and fat accumulated in the burger and fries. Calvin thanked the person who created the Meal Deal. Now Calvin could balance the fat and starch with empty calories and somehow feel good about it. As he took a quick handful of fries and stuffed them into his mouth in one giant shove, he pulled out of the drive-thru and away from the Burger Barn.

The office complex where Calvin worked was only two blocks away, which meant it would take only about a minute to get from one place to the other on normal two-way streets. Unfortunately, the streets were one-way only and forced him to go right instead of left to the office. Calvin was then forced to travel two more blocks before finding a one-way street right, which would lead to another one-way street back to the office.

As Calvin turned onto the first street out of the Burger Barn, it took him longer than expected to get to his next right turn. Traffic seemed bad for some reason. As he finally made the right turn, Calvin understood why. A crane was holding a billboard that had been posted on the left side of the road. No buildings had been present in the middle of town since the owners had chosen to use advertising instead of concrete to make their mark. Thinking back, Calvin could not remember ever actually reading the sign, much less remembering it, but he shrugged it off.

The workers seemed active. One man was yelling into his radio and his hand signals showed he was talking about the sign. Someone on the ground was yelling at the man in the crane, who couldn't hear and was motioning that he could not. Calvin looked back and forth at the men and wondered whatever happened to the Three Stooges. They really should bring those shows back.

The commotion and the lack of movement from the cars in front of him caused Calvin to look up and see what the commotion was all about. A sign advertising the latest Godzilla movie was swinging overhead. The sign appeared to have somehow come unattached from the base poles and was being maneuvered back into place. Three men were atop a platform, holding onto ropes attached to the sign trying to maneuver it back into place so that they could attach it to the posts. The problem was that the sign was swinging like a seesaw, up and down on each side. An extremely upset-looking lizard stood next to the words: "Save yourselves! Godzilla is coming! Cities and People in his path are all doomed! Calvin had grown up on old Godzilla and other monster movies. He could only hope that this new Godzilla was better than the last over-hyped one they'd created a few years ago. He also hoped the director would have Godzilla take down King Kong. The thought of an oversized ape beating the largest mutant reptile ever was ridiculous in Calvin's mind.

A car horn snapped Calvin back to the road in front of him; the cars had begun to move ahead and a gap had formed between himself and the car ahead. Calvin took a quick look up to see that the sign had stopped moving and decided everything was okay. Besides, these were professionals hanging the sign.

It happened in an instant. As soon as he pushed the car forward, a loud cracking sound echoed throughout the area. Calvin looked at the man who was talking on the radio. He had dropped the radio and was running down the street, as was the man he'd been talking to. Calvin never let off the gas, he continued to coast towards the traffic that was leaving him behind. Then suddenly the billboard dropped onto the street just feet beyond Calvin's front bumper, splintering and ripping into several pieces. Calvin slammed on the brakes with all his might. He stopped just in time to avoid getting a chunk of the billboard sign dropped directly on top of him. The piece was larger than the hood of his car that had just missed hitting him by a few feet.

Standing steadfast in front of him, in a perfectly upright position was the middle of the sign. Somehow, the sign had separated into three sections from the crane and had fallen to earth with a crash. The other two sections had fallen on either side of the road and slammed face down. The middle had become caught up on the chain it was dangling from in mid-air and had flipped end over end to its resting place, a few feet in front of Calvin's bumper, but that was not what was making Calvin's heart pound. For all the fear that the moment should have brought, Calvin acknowledged none of it.

Calvin neither moved, nor blinked for several minutes. Other drivers who had witnessed the event had come running to his car to see if he was okay. The workers had regained their ground and returned to the scene and saw Calvin. They too went to see if he was okay. Several people pounded on the window, others were staring at him, wondering if he was in shock or just too scared to move.

Calvin stared ahead in disbelief. There was no pounding, no noise, nothing. There was only the sign in front of him. The sign had broken so perfectly that only a few of the words had fallen together. He read it again in disbelief. There before him read the words "Save Godz People."

13

The first day of school was usually the most exciting day of the year. Students meeting friends that they hadn't seen since school let out over two months ago. The fact that they promised to call each other and hang out all summer was long ago and quite forgotten. Now it was all about the new clothes and hairstyles that each of them sported.

Of course the girls were the ones who spoke directly about it, the boys just made fun of the other boys who had cooler shirts.

The teachers were equally excited about this time of the year. They had been in faculty meetings for almost a week, learning exactly nothing. After the first day of the fancy rhetoric, most teachers assumed the school district had hired the voice-over for the teacher in the Peanuts cartoon; "Wa, wawa wa wu," was pretty much all they heard. The teachers were only given two hours of time to work in their rooms and prepare for a year with students. because of this, the first day was usually very disorganized.

Janiyah had been longing for this day. She'd had to sit in the doctor's room or in her room at the hospital too many times and had day-dreamed about her normal life. She dreamt of the time when she could walk down the hallways and talk to her friends, look at boys (well, maybe), and actually go to class. The last part surprised Janiyah the most. She knew she had always liked to learn, but never realized that she actually enjoyed going to class.

Today, however, she felt more like Moses than a freshman in high school. As soon as she'd arrived at the school, the murmurs and whispers had begun. As Janiyah made her way through the halls, the other students spread out to each wall as fast as possible. A sea of Hollister and Fossil separated as she walked down the hallway.

It was all she could do to not cry. However, there was something inside Janiyah that wouldn't allow it. She would not show emotion today. She had fought too hard to come back to a normal life to allow it to fall apart now. The doctors had warned Janiyah that this might happen. Most of the students would know she had a breakdown, or "gone crazy" as the kids would describe it, but most would not know all of what happened. They would hear a rumor and would of course fill in their own blanks.

When Janiyah turned the corner to the science labs, her heart skipped a beat. There in the middle of a group of girls that were trying desperately to walk away from her was one of her best friends, Tonya. She had not called nor written Janiyah the entire time away and was now physically trying to distance herself. Unfortunately, it did not stop their voices from carrying.

"Did she really go crazy?" asked one of the lackeys.

"Totally," Tonya replied.

"Why?" Lackey number two asked as she tried to peer over her shoulder at Janiyah, who stood watching the entire performance.

"Nobody knows, but I heard she was hearing voices," said the now-popular Tonya.

Her group stopped and looked at her as if she had just predicted the winning lottery tickets for the next ten years. It was the strain in their necks that Janiyah noticed. Each one of the girls was desperately trying not to look back at her as they forced their attention onto Tonya. Either they were scared to look at the spooky-voices girl, or they were too afraid not to look at Tonya. Tonya took their looks as a sign that they were too mesmerized by her to look away. Her perceived newfound popularity won out, so she did what any other teenage girl that had absolutely no clue what she was talking about did: She kept talking about it.

"Seriously," she said. Another great teenage line signifying that she was not all that serious. "I heard that she heard so many voices that she went totally loony and had to be restrained. I'm surprised they let her out."

"Actually . . . ." Janiyah's voice caught them off guard. She had walked up to them while their strained necks were diverted to Tonya, who was now standing directly behind them.

With a start, they turned in horror to look at Janiyah as if she were some deranged monster meant to be locked away, which of course was exactly what they were thinking.

"Actually," she continued again with their attention, "there was only one voice and it was your mom's, Tonya. She was asking me to please help you with your food problem. Apparently, you can't turn away anything." Janiyah made a gesture with her eyes to look around the crowd at Tonya's butt. Janiyah shoots and scores!

"Whatever," the witty banter from Tonya continued. "Let's go, girls. Psycho needs therapy."

As the girls turned abruptly and walked away, Janiyah felt a sense of shame. She knew she should be the bigger person, but Tonya had been a friend and now turned on her. It was the first time she had confronted anyone about it, and she felt worse than she thought she would have.

"Don't worry about her," a voice said from behind her.

Janiyah didn't have to turn around. She knew that voice and it carried a weight of relief that Jessica would never have realized.

"She's been acting all weird the entire summer. Apparently she claims she was only friends with us out of pity."

Janiyah turned to look at Jessica, who was staring knives into the backs of Tonya and her cronies. Finally she stopped and looked at Janiyah and smiled. "What's up?" she asked in an only-friends-get-it, small-talk, all-is-okay kind of way.

"Oh, you know," Janiyah began but abruptly stopped herself. With Jessica, she could just be herself. With a sigh of relief, she pushed Tonya and the cronies out of her mind and focused on Jessica. "Hey," she began again, "what class do you have first period?"

"Chemistry with Mr. Reagan. What about you?"

"Chemistry, but I have Ms. Pope."

The two looked a little down for not having the same class.

"Well, at least we are close to each other," Jessica said as she grabbed Janiyah's arm to walk with her down the hall. "Ms. Pope is supposed to be really cool. You'll like her."

And with that, the two friends moved off down the hall and all was right in the world of teenage angst, at least for one period.

14

The storm exited the corner office and began to gain momentum. Every step added to the thunder as lightning raged overhead. Quickly, people dove out of the way to save themselves from the onslaught even though the eye of the storm was not focused on them—they simple dove for freedom. The storm turned down the second row of cubicles, passing Karli without even a glance.

Karli was magically able to disappear behind the handset of a telephone that was now ringing "Please make a call or try again."

The storm was now at full steam, turned its last turn, and stood in the final cubicle of the second row. Lights flashed, thunder struck, and small towns were eliminated from the face of the earth.

In a phrase, Candace was pissed.

"I asked you for the Oklahoma numbers over two hours ago and your budget is due today. I need that budget to finalize our requests," Candace screeched as if Calvin couldn't hear her from the two feet that separated them. "You have been staring out the window all afternoon and I need those numbers."

Calvin almost replied that there are no windows in cubicles and he would have to stand up just to be able to see a window much less look out of one, but he had a fear of tornadoes in tight spaces.

"Sorry, I had my thoughts on Louisiana," Captain Cover-up replied as he made a mental note to prepare something new for Louisiana at some point in the next week.

"I need all of it before you leave today. Thanks." The last part screeched more of a Do It Now or feel lightning reach places you did not know you had. And, with that, the storm turned and flew back to its office amid scorched earth, fire, and the heavy sighs of fellow workers glad they were not the cause of it.

George looked over the cubicle with a huge smile that held back laughter. "Didn't you say we weren't looking at Louisiana for another two months?"

"Hey, it was short notice," Calvin replied with smile.

George returned to his cubicle lest the storm return for him.

Calvin had been unable to work all afternoon. Thoughts about the billboard had given way to the voice of the airport, which of course led to the memory of the train tracks. Calvin now felt as though he stood atop a fence. Either he could fall onto the coincidence side and save much humiliation while keeping the pain of failing inside; or he could fall onto the second-chance side, which admitted the voices were real, and he was either crazy or chosen for something that he was not prepared for. Either way, Calvin was scared to death.

It took until the late hours of the evening for Calvin to tally his numbers, correct his budget, and actually focus on finishing his work. The storm had left, stating that she would be finishing the worksheets at home if Calvin had the decency to complete his assigned tasks. Thank God for email, Calvin thought—actually handing in paper budgets to her after nightfall was more than he cared to imagine.

Finally, with moon and stars over his head, Calvin was able to leave. When he reached his car, he realized he was trying to put his wife's key into his car door. As he tried to balance a briefcase in his left hand and change keys in his right hand, he lost control of the key chain and it dropped to the ground. That coincided almost immediately with a direct downpour that came out of nowhere. Here, thought Calvin, was the icing on the cake.

Calvin was finally able to get into his car and sit down with a splash. Once the car was running and the windshield wipers turned on, he was able to see just how hard it was raining. There was barely any visibility ten feet in front of him, and he wasn't even driving yet. Facing the choice of either going home in torrential downpour barely able to see where he was going or who was around him or stay in the parking lot of his office and risk Candace's return, Calvin started up the car and drove home.

International Tech had built a small maintenance building in the middle of a grassy field with electric wires and poles surrounding it in all directions. A small white pickup with the word MAINTENANCE was parked close to the building. The building's roof was on fire; flames were shooting out of it. Inside were two men, one older and unconscious, and one younger and scared to death.

The small building was surrounded by a fence that stretched for miles in either direction, with no gates in sight. The main complex was miles off.

Nobody could touch the fence. The spectators knew this since the first man had run to the fence to yell for help, touched the fence, and had shocked himself into a long nap.

All of this was taking place just off Highway 635, just past the onramp but far enough off that the drivers on the highway could slow down and look, but not pull over. Only those coming from the onramp had a chance to stop without getting rear-ended. A few had made the effort to pull over to help.

The shack's door was blocked by a metal pole that had fallen on top of Darryl, the older man, and hit him square on the head. The pole now lay across the door, keeping it from being opened. The windows were engulfed in flames and Jackson, the younger maintenance worker, was beginning to lose his breath. The electric fence that surrounded International Tech's perimeter was holding strong—unfortunately for the workers.

Several onlookers outside the fence were discouraged by what they were watching and their inability to help. The rain was coming down hard, as were the lighting strikes, one of which had begun this fiasco with the little shack. The storm itself was gaining in its intensity. Each onlooker cursed the weather and his or her idleness. People were using their cell phones to call IT's offices to get them out here, or at least shut down the electricity to the fence. Too many people were calling and the lines were beginning to jam. The operator for IT had just left for the day; however, if the onlookers wanted to leave a message someone would get back with them shortly.

Calvin had already pulled over once. His windshield wiper had become loose and instead of wiping water off the windshield, it was banging on the hood and the roof in steady rhythmic beats. Calvin had to pull over on the side of the street amid horns honking and fingers being displayed. After getting the wiper fixed, Calvin was able to literally slide into his seat. It felt like a Slip 'N Slide as he tried to maneuver his body back to his seated position. The feel of wet underwear underneath a dripping suit was almost as uncomfortable as the cold air of the a/c blowing on him. Calvin quickly turned off the a/c, which fogged up the windshield in front of him.

Eventually, Calvin was able to see out of the front windshield enough that he could begin to drive again. Calvin reached Interstate 635, after cutting off a Ford F-250 as he worked his way back onto the street. He had to go under the bridge to reach his onramp, which was difficult now that the Ford was directly behind him with its headlights shining directly into Calvin's car. The truck's driver must have decided that Calvin couldn't see well enough and had turned on the brights in order to aid in Calvin's already wonderful driving experience. Calvin assumed that the Ford's driver was using his finger as well.

As Calvin reached the onramp, his windshield wiper began to teeter as if it were about to fall off again. He would have pulled over to fix it, but there were too many cars on the shoulder to pull over and Mr. Ford behind him was driving as close to Calvin as possible. He was just about to reach the end of the cars when the Ford accelerated and roared by him and then swerved right into Calvin's path, cutting Calvin off.

At the exact same time, lighting struck and hit a transformer knocking out the electricity in the area and for two more blocks past.

Calvin was forced to swerve to avoid hitting the truck, which sent him hydroplaning and simultaneously knocking loose his windshield wiper. Calvin straightened his car, but could not see which way was straight. A a loud clash and the simultaneous bouncing of him six inches off his seat told him he was not on the highway, and he was picking up speed as the car went downhill. He was about to hit his brakes as a metallic scraping reverberated through his car. Frozen in panic, Calvin finally realized he needed to stop his car. He hit the brakes and finally came to a sliding stop. He jumped out of his car and fell flat on his face in mud.

Later, many of the onlookers would praise the maintenance workers' savior. The driver had apparently cared little for his own safety as he took out an electric fence with his common-looking car—it was hard to tell exactly what kind it was with the power off—but drove directly through the fence and to the shack. The all saw a man fall out of his vehicle, and race to the shack, only to find it locked. He then used his car to break it down and pull the men to safety.

The facts were that Calvin was in a panic. Once the mud cleared from his eyes, he realized he was on private property and had destroyed their fence. Assuming it was IT's, he knew he was in it deep. He quickly got back in his car, but it wouldn't move. After stomping on the gas repeatedly, he was able to get a slight movement and turn the steering wheel. The car began to move, then lurched forward and slid. Stuck again, Calvin gassed it, but to no use.

His panic increased and Calvin decided to try reverse. It worked easily as the car escaped the mud but slammed directly into a tiny shack. The door, now wide open, along with almost the entire wall, Calvin looked back and saw flames everywhere. First the fence, then the grass, now a building. Boy, was he in trouble now.

It was at this moment that he saw movement in his rearview mirror. Someone was waving his arms. Calvin tried to open his door, but it was jammed shut. The man was coming toward him carrying something big. Calvin squinted to see. It was another man. Oh, man, had he hit him? Oh, he was really in trouble now. The man grabbed the trunk of the car and was yelling. Calvin couldn't hear, but could see his face. The man was scared.

Calvin hit the gas and the car escaped the rubble with the man holding on for dear life. Finally, Calvin stopped at a point when he knew they would be safe. He climbed out of the passenger door again, and again fell face first in mud. He quickly got upright and walked back to the man, expecting the worst.

Another man ran past Calvin to the figure lying on the ground and picked him up.

"God bless you, God bless you," was all the younger man was saying.

Other shouts were coming from the hill as people began flocking towards them.

"You saved us. The lighting caught us off guard and you came anyway. Thank you," a young, rather scared guy with "Maintenance" stenciled into his shirt pocket was saying as he clutched an older man in his arms.

"You mean I didn't do that?" Calvin asked, more to himself than the man.

"The lighting must have hit the building. When it did, one of the beams fell right on top of Randall. He's out cold, but still breathing. I was almost out when you knocked the door down. Who are you?"

The last question came and went without Calvin hearing. He hadn't caused the accident; he had saved them. Calvin was beginning to like the idea of having saved someone when the shouts came closer and shook him from his thoughts. It was at that time he realized that his car had the back bumper bent and mud stuck everywhere and the driver-side doors were both dented in. He also realized he was trespassing.

"Uh, I gotta go!" he shouted and climbed back in the car through the passenger seat. As the people began to surround the scene, Calvin panicked. *What if one of them called IT,* was his fearful thought. With his foot on the gas, Calvin fishtailed, causing everyone to jump aside. The car then caught hold of the ground and he sped off across the lawn, spewing mud all over the spectators and a very young, scared, and now confused and muddy maintenance worker.

Calvin's car sped up the hill, then across the shoulder, and turned onto the highway, cutting off a motorcycle in doing so. The spectators watched with a mix of awe and confusion.

"Who was he? He just saved those people and he leaves?"

Another replied, "I don't know; there was mud all over his face. But that was cool."

Finally another, "Yeah, it was, but does he realize he has part of the fence attached to his bumper?"

The spectators looked down the highway and watched as sparks lit up the night and the beaten-up old sedan drive away with a piece of fence attached to the bumper. Ten seconds later, the sparks ended with a crash as the bumper and the attached fence piece fell off in the middle of a lane on I635.

15

He had no longer sat down in his cruiser, when the radio chirped. He was being sent to an accident off highway I635 where some lunatic had just cut off a motorcyclist, who was now stuck in a ditch, and there was a maintenance building on fire and the security gate was totally destroyed. Put all that in a list with the heavy downpour and you could say Tommy Ray was in for a long night.

Tommy Ray had been with the force for almost eight years. He'd come straight out of high school to the force. He had worked hard at moving up, including graduating from college. Once he had his degree, he'd been promoted out of traffic, to detective. Now, instead of pulling over speeders, he was pulling them out of ditches and finding out why they were there in the first place.

As he drove under the bridge and turned onto the onramp that would take him to the highway, Tommy Ray saw a chaotic scene. There on the right were five cars parked on the shoulder. Several paces down the shoulder were an ambulance and a fire truck. Another police cruiser from Traffic was ahead of them. To the right of the shoulder was a hill that led down into a slight ditch, only the ditch smoothed out to flat land the closer it led backward where the parked cars overlooked it. Tommy Ray parked close to the ambulance and got out to look at the scene, instantly soaked by the squall that still pounded the land.

There was a motorcycle in the ditch, some foreign kind Tommy Ray believed by the look of it: yellow with black stripes, and now L-shaped. Presumably, it was the driver who was being carried out on a stretcher. An officer was following the victim out of the ditch and spotted Tommy Ray standing there. With a nod of his head, he turned and came up to Tommy Ray.

Tommy Ray turned to his right and looked to the other field that was IT's private land. There was a metal fence with a ripped hole in it. Wheel tracks led down the hill straight through the fence and into a field where there were people talking to another officer next to what used to be a building. It was still smoking even in this downpour, so Tommy Ray assumed it had just burned down. There were tire tracks all around the front of the smoldering shack. Apparently, the officer questioning the witnesses did not get the concept of protecting the scene.

"Lightning strike," the officer said as he panted up the hill, water dripping off the plastic tip of his hat.

"What about these car marks?" Tommy Ray asked.

"There were two guys locked in the building. A bunch of people out here could see them through a window, but it was pretty much engulfed in flames," the officer said.

Tommy Ray took a glance at his name badge: Officer Steven Florez, then began walking down the hill toward the scene with Florez following alongside.

The officer continued his story. "So, the fence is lit up like a Christmas tree so nobody could get close to it. The two men were goners."

"Were the two men working for IT?"

"Yes, both were maintenance workers. So, one guy gets a cracked scalp and he's out. The other is losing it and cannot find a way out. Nobody can clear the fence. That's when this guy shows up."

"The one who made the tire marks?" Tommy Ray pointed to the tire tracks that circled around them as the two men arrived at an open space in front of the former maintenance shack.

"Uh-huh. This guy decides to take the fence out with his car, only the lightning got there first. Whammo!" The officer described the lightning strike as he clapped his hands together and then spread his arms into a giant Y. "The lightning hits a transformer and the gate is off. The guy takes out the gate and flies down here."

"And then what?" Tommy Ray looked at the bystanders watching him and Florez from behind a police tape.

"Well, according to the onlookers, this guy spins his car around and then backs in right through the door to the building."

This got Tommy Ray's attention. He had been listening, but was more set to look at the scene rather than hear the story. He turned his attention to Florez, who began to show more interest in the story.

"That's right. He drove straight into the door and took it out. Then one of the workers grabs hold of the trunk lid with one hand and his buddy with the other and this guy pulls him out to safety."

"Where is he?"

"That's just the thing. He took off. Nobody got a license plate because the mud covered up almost everything. A few people got a look, but he was so muddy, nobody could get a clear look at his face."

"And the motorcycle?"

"Well, when the guy took off, he popped back onto the on ramp and fishtailed out of here. A piece of the gate was stuck to the bumper. When he hit the ramp, the guy on the motorcycle was cut off and had to cut sharply not to hit the gate. He flew into the ditch. Good thing the rain has been pouring though; it made the ground soft for his landing. The good thing is that it happened in the first place."

"Oh, and why is that?" Tommy Ray asked.

A Voice from the Restroom

"Because, the guy on the motorcycle is Bob Jung. He's wanted in Oklahoma for aggravated assault and several speeding violations. No one could catch him on that bike of his until now."

Tommy Ray thanked Florez for the report. He looked around the scene to reflect on what he had to work with. A guy saves two lives and takes off, only to nearly take out a guy on a motorcycle who turns up wanted. No license, no face, and all he had was just the size and exploits of the man. This was a strange situation.

A light had turned on behind Tommy Ray, a flashing light on top of a small truck. Getting out was a security guard who Tommy Ray assumed worked for IT and a man in a nice suit that was getting soaked fast. When they reached him, the suit moved past the security guard and directly into Tommy Ray's face.

"I am Gale Myers and I am the lead attorney for IT." He stopped and looked at the name badge. "Mr. Ray, we will need to be involved in everything that happens on our property."

"Detective Tommy Ray Hudson. I am handling this investigation." The suit appeared unhappy at the statement. He took Tommy Ray's hand and shoved his slightly wet card into it.

"Please escort these people off our property. I'm sure you can ask those questions somewhere else."

"Certainly, once we are done with our investigation," Tommy Ray replied, giving the man a stare that said the conversation was over. The suit sounded off a slight "humph" and turned to get back into the truck. Tommy Ray turned and looked at the scene again. The man with no face who'd saved two lives and nearly wrecked another man, one the police had been looking for. Now, the IT suit-man was pushing Tommy Ray to be involved in the case. Oh, yeah, and the crime scene was a mess, too.

16

For Benjamin Hawkins, it was the research and planning that made it work. For Jerold McNeill, it was the idea. Of course, neither of them liked getting up early in the morning, especially after a late night on the Xbox360 playing Halo. For Jerry, it was even harder. He usually couldn't see the importance of knowing exactly where to go and when to be there. It was assumed that he would just find the right place when it came to him. Ben, on the other hand, was always trying to get it exactly right. That was usually why Ben was stuck up in a dark pipe or small storage area. Ben planned things out, Jerry could wing it. Ben was the talker, Jerry the cover.

Today was a different story. The school had finished a new wing that housed most of the Arts department including the new auditorium. Neither knew the layout very well. They each woke up early and ready for the research, a nice thought for Ben, since he didn't have to hear Jerry whine. With Starbucks in hand, they parked close to the school so that they could see the side and rear entrances facing the street. It was important to know which doors came in and out of.

They waited for the students to begin coming to school as they finished drawing a map of the outside on white printer paper, the doors and possible entrance windows being well marked. They penciled in the storm ladder that rode the east wall to the roof, albeit a little darker than the marks for the doors or windows. Once the students began to arrive, stars were put on the spots that were used to allow entrance into the early day school. It wasn't very clever, but it served the purpose for Ben and Jerry.

With their calculations done, Ben began to drive off and Jerry began to whine.

"Where is she? Did you see her?"

"No," Ben replied. He wasn't expecting to find the victim they were hunting for, but it didn't matter. However, he was worried about Jerry wanting to find her. They needed to move slowly on this and Jerry tended to get a little excited and act too quickly.

"She's there and there's time," Ben said.

"We've been paying for her attitude too long we gotta get her again," Jerry continued. "She's gotta be here!"

"She will be, but don't worry now. We will get her when the time is right."

Jerry didn't like it, but he sat back in his seat anyway and began to relax. "Okay, but her time is coming. Again."

17

Darkness crept up as the lights flickered on in the light posts and the neon signs. Calvin sat inside the plush interior of his new Yaris, barely noticing the change in the time. The car he sat in registered only fifty-four miles and reminded Calvin of the cars that the clowns drove in the circus, only there dozens of clowns popped out. Here, Calvin could barely imagine another person fitting in with him. It did have that new car smell, but Calvin figured that would last only until he picked up his first hamburger at a drive-thru.

But none of that mattered to Calvin right now. He sat in the car, staring at the building in front of him. There were only two other cars in the vast parking lot and they were parked directly in front of the building. Calvin sat sufficiently far away, underneath a light post whose light bulb had burned out.

He looked at the sign on the building. It was the reason he'd come here in the first place. The top of the sign had St. Mary's name on it, but it was not the name of the church, but the message under it that had caught Calvin's attention. "Come and speak to our preacher anytime!" Calvin had wanted to talk with someone. He needed someone to tell him this was just a coincidence, a joke, but he feared the other answer that might come.

Becca had waited up for Calvin last night. She had begun to fall asleep when the electricity had shut off. That wasn't so much the problem as what followed. Josten, the family's eleven-year-old Golden Retriever, had started to, in Becca's words, freak out. For some dogs, it was vacuum cleaners, others it was whistles, but for Josten, it was the high-pitched chirp of the smoke alarms signaling they were off line.

What was unexplainable was where Josten would run. The bathtub had thwarted Josten's existence for a happy life for eleven years. There were plenty of treats, walks, back rubs, and even her own fluffy bed with her private toys on it. She was always well fed and loved by these two-legged friends of hers. But that vile white contraption that spewed water and engulfed her every other week was just too much. Josten would run, scratch, tremble, shake, and whine when she was dragged to it, but the bathtub and her owner would defeat her every time.

And yet, that was where Josten ran to when the smoke alarms went off. The vile contraption that devoured the hard-earned dirt and mud that Josten loved so much now became her safe haven and protective fort.

Becca could deal with Josten running to the tub, and she could even handle the pitter-patter of Josten's nails as the stepped in circles, searching for a way to make the madness of the chirping stop. What she couldn't deal with was the banging in the walls. Josten was blind, but Becca either didn't realize it or failed to acknowledge it. Josten was Josten and that was that.

So, as the smoke alarms chirped, Josten took off for the bathtub in such a sprint that most colleges would award her a scholarship just to join their track team. Then, in the same instance, a loud bang would follow the sprint as Josten ran head first into the wall. By now, Josten's head was strong enough to withstand walls, concrete, and possibly even World War III. So, Josten just stood back up, and ran for the tub again. After three more thuds, Josten reached the comfort of the bathtub and began her prance.

By the time Calvin reached home minus the rear bumper, Becca was in such a fuss over the smoke alarm and Josten that Calvin decided not to bother her with the car. After a sleepless night, Calvin got out of bed early and left for work before the sun or any human presence was awake.

Candace, on the other hand, was a completely different story. After an almost half hour tirade on what was Calvin thinking by not getting his work done, and by destroying company property and why he was evil since he was born a man and how the entire office was slacking and he was a prime example, Calvin was finally allowed to call about getting a loan car. Unfortunately, the only car available was a two-door Yaris. Oh, the excitement.

After spending five minutes just trying to get his body in the driver's-side door, Calvin drove off the lot and nearly into a moving van coming directly at him. It was a little difficult to turn the wheel as Calvin's belly blocked any attempt to properly grip the wheel. Finally, after forcing the gas and revving the engine, Calvin was able to reach nearly forty miles per hour after only half a minute.

He'd spent the remainder of the day dodging Hurricane Candace and trying vainly to actually do his job. It seemed the entire office wanted to know what happened, but never at the same time. Not wanting to let everyone know that he had destroyed a high profile companies land and nearly drove backwards into two men in a shack, he decided to make something up. Calvin had told and retold his made-up story so much so that it almost started sounding convincing.

Poor Calvin had been trying to get to work, but the traffic had been so bad that it forced Calvin to take a back road he was unfamiliar with. At a four way stop sign, Calvin stopped, looked both ways and then began to move forward and was almost across the intersection when a truck sped forth from out of nowhere and ran the stop sign. Calvin had been forced to accelerate quickly to miss the truck, but a dog ran across the street at that precise time. Calvin swerved, but the speed was too great and it forced him to slide into the ditch running parallel with the street. His rear bumper saved him but took the brunt of the fall. Of course the dog was safe. Somehow though, Calvin thought the dog had changed from a bloodhound to a Weimaraner, but he wasn't too sure. By the end of the story, Calvin decided it was too quick to have seen what kind. It must have been a mutt.

Calvin had decided to take a different route home than usual. Maybe his story had given him the idea, maybe he just needed time to think or maybe he didn't want to see any police cars follow him without a missing bumper. He wasn't exactly sure, but he knew he needed some time alone to think and taking back roads to get home would at least give him some extra time..

As Calvin drove his thoughts became a mixture of regret, shock and lack of understanding of what had happened to him to get him where he was today. The thoughts clouded his mind so much that he drove further than he expected into an area he did not recognize. He decided to turn around and go back from where he came, but it took him nearly a mile to find a spot to turn around. As he did, a church with an enormous neon sign caught his attention. After searching for answers, one now showed up in a neon sign before him.

As he stared up at the sign, waiting for something to happen, Calvin began to shake. The memories of failing and almost letting his friend die, the voice that seemed so real then and now the voice that seemed so real in the restroom all began to weigh on him. Nothing made sense and Calvin was afraid of the answers. Maybe it was his fear, or maybe it was what might be said, or maybe it was just sitting in that parking lot thinking of too many possibilities, but something in Calvin was not ready for the answers. Not yet. Calvin turned on the car and began to drive away. He stopped to look up at the neon sign and half expected it to come crashing down on him.

Well, he thought, at least it wasn't a fifty-foot lizard.

18

Janiyah closed her algebra book and placed it in her backpack. She had been doing homework for two hours straight and was exhausted. After crawling into bed, she was finally able to put a perspective on the day she'd had. The stares and the whispers had followed her everywhere she'd gone. It was exceptionally hard in Chemistry and Algebra since her seat was in the front row where everybody could see her. In these classes, the whispers were amplified, tearing at her with every stab. Fortunately, Ms. Pope realized what was happening and moved her to the side of the room next to the window. With all eyes staring forward, there was less attention on Janiyah here.

The rest of the day had gone as expected. The seas would part as Janiyah walked down the halls. Whispers and finger-pointing continued and the occasional boy, trying to look cool for his friends or girlfriend, would make a comment, trying to look impressive. Janiyah's favorite one was "Janiyah, God wants you to build an ark." She wasn't sure if she was allowed to laugh at her own expense, but it did lighten her mood.

Fortunately, there was Jessica. The two of them met and stayed together as much as they could. When school was over, they waited inside Ms. Pope's room just a little while longer, asking questions about the lecture that they already knew. Janiyah felt that Ms. Pope knew what they were doing, but answered the questions happily as if she was glad to help. Finally, the day was over, and the two girls walked out of the school to a quiet day.

After crossing the street and walking home quickly in order to not meet any more would be fans, the two girls were able to settle down and talk about their favorite thing: Boys. All in all, it was a tough day, but nothing that Janiyah hadn't expected. Besides, she thought, there were only 179 more days of this. No sweat! And with that, she rolled over and went to sleep.

19

It was a special presentation of *Monday Night Football on ESPN*. The special part being that it was Thursday and the NFL was enough. The game was on, but Calvin didn't really care. Too much had gone on lately for him to keep his mind on any one thing. Usually the Dallas Cowboys playing in Washington was enough to ignite a fire Cowboy enthusiasm; tonight, though, his thoughts were elsewhere. Becca had already come in and scolded him for Josten's "little gift" being left in the dining room. He wasn't sure how he had any control of Josten's bowels, but he dutifully took the point without a flinch.

Between work, kids, PTA's, homework help, and basically life in general, Calvin and Becca had little time together just to themselves. The Cowboys playing was one of the few times the kids gave them space. With three television sets in the house, Adam could play Madden Football on the Xbox, Maureen could see her ten-thousandth episode of *Witches of Waverly Place* and Calvin and Becca could regain the living room together. Seeing that Calvin was not into the game like he was on other nights, Becca took the moment to tell him about her newly read book. Calvin missed the name but it had something to do with mutual funds and their relationship to communism, poverty and Milk

Duds. As Becca explained the book to him, Calvin drifted off in his own thoughts of recent events and mildly back to the football game. It was the mention of Milk Duds that brought Calvin back to interest, but Becca ended the oration stating it was time to get the kids to bed.   Now, alone again, Calvin was left with the fourth rerun of a Wendy's commercial and his own thoughts. Somewhere, deep inside him, Calvin kept hearing the same voice. He knew the pitch, the tone, and even the slight lisp of the words. Finally, reluctantly, Calvin closed his eyes and pictured the scene again.

He hadn't smiled, laughed, and had barely spoken for a month. His parents were worried and had asked the school counselor to speak with him. When Calvin hadn't spoken to her, she told his parents that he needed professional help. That was when they turned to Reverend Clark.

For almost a week now, Calvin had sat in the same office, an hour at a time, listening to the good Reverend speak to him, pleading with Calvin to talk with him. The office was roomy by business standards, much less for a church. Calvin sat in a leather arm chair that seemed to swallow him from its size. The pastor sat behind an ornate mahogany desk with a gold plate with the good reverend's name on it. A gold cross sat on one side of the name plate, with a pen and holder sitting on the other side. The room was full of pictures of the pastor with various people in exotic places that Calvin could only guess at. A few golf pictures and religious quotes had been framed and placed sporadically throughout the office. Reverend Clark would rarely move from behind the desk, but chose different times to stand and speak when he was trying to make a point. Eventually though, as if his restraints had been broken down enough to breathe or he was just plain tired of being silent, Calvin spoke up.

"I tried to save him, I really did, but I just couldn't move," Calvin burst out in the middle of Reverend Clark's speech about honoring his mother and father.

"What did you say?" the good reverend replied.

"I tried to save him. God told me to. I heard him. God said to save him, to save his people, but I couldn't move. I was too scared."

The look on the reverend's face was more of fear than a question. With more of a squeak than a voice, he asked Calvin to explain.

Calvin told the man how he and Martin had played so often on the train tracks. He began crying when he said he saw Martin caught with his arm in the tracks and how the train was coming fast. Then he tried to explain how the voice came to him, but he could never get it quite right, but he remembered what it said: He was to save Martin. But he couldn't move. Calvin had a full flood of tears bursting when he exclaimed about being too scared and how he turned away and thought Martin was dead because of him. But Martin was alive and fine and Calvin knew he had failed. Now Martin was moving away and Calvin was left alone with the guilt.

For the first time in a long time, Calvin felt better. He had finally opened up and said that he had heard God and to a man who would believe him.

The good reverend didn't speak again for a few moments and then stood up, walked around the desk, and sat next to Calvin on an equally plush leather chair.

"Calvin," the reverend started, his voice a little shaky, "sometimes we confuse our conscience with a voice."

"But I heard him!"

"Calvin," Reverend Clark forcibly spoke again. "You are upset about failing God because you believe you heard him speak." The reverend put up his hand, keeping Calvin from interjecting. "You feel guilty, which is understandable. But do not compare your conscience with the actual voice of God." With that, he stood and walked back to his chair on the far side of the desk.

Calvin sat in shock. How could the reverend not believe him? Of all people, why not him? This is why he hadn't wanted to speak to anyone about it; it sounded too crazy. "But, sir," Calvin said, "*I* believe it was God's voice."

"Then you failed him, Calvin."

Calvin could barely breathe as the time passed. It seemed like decades eroded before Calvin had the nerve to speak again. "Will he give me a second chance?"

The reverend looked Calvin in the eye with astonishment, and then looked away toward a picture of him and a friend on a rather green golf course next to an ocean. "If God wants you again, then I guess he will speak to you," the reverend snapped.

Slowly the reality of the situation hit Calvin as he sat once again in front of the television. The Cowboys had scored two more times and Calvin's face had flooded with tears. He knew the reverend hadn't believed him and hadn't wanted anything to do with him. He never again spoke to the reverend and eventually, once he became an adult, stopped going to church. It wasn't until he got married that he began again, and that was only to appease Becca.

Josten walked in and sat next to Calvin, practically on his feet. As Calvin bent down to pet her, he could only think of one thing. God had not spoken to him since that day, at least, not until the airport. Why was he speaking to him now?

20

It had been a sleepless night. Most nights were lately. Tommy Ray was a morning person, mainly because it focused on the day at hand. Nights carried too much weight, especially when he hadn't talked to Daniel. But this morning, it was a little rougher than usual.

It had all started at work. He had received a new assignment, since the fiasco at IT was not going anywhere. There had been a series of pranks played out in the area and other jurisdictions were contacting each other to gather information. Tommy Ray had been chosen to assist in the investigation and had subsequently been on the phone for nearly six hours straight. After the last call, he was able to get an hour in the weight room before calling it a night.

He walked into an empty apartment. Tommy Ray had walked home to an empty apartment for three years. Sarah had divorced him, saying he was too involved in his job and never had time for her. Sometimes, she would say, that he would bring the frustration of work home with him. Of course, Tommy Ray would reply that was what being a detective was all about and she knew that when they married. She didn't care, she just wanted out. Tommy Ray wasn't sure but he suspected she had been cheating on him for quite awhile before that. If he had cared enough, he might have said something. He didn't.

What he did care about was their son Daniel. Two weeks before signing the divorce papers, everything was shaky. The settlement had been hard fought, but there was equal time split between parents. Tommy Ray and Sarah each had ammo to use against the other, Tommy Ray had her boyfriend if he needed it, Sarah could use his job. They were set to meet one more time with lawyers and settle the matter and sign the papers and Tommy Ray would be free with his son, at least half the time. He was happy. He didn't mind losing Sarah, but it would crush him to lose his son.

That day, a call came in that a robbery had taken place in an uptown apartment complex, and Tommy Ray had been assigned to it. It seemed like a pretty obvious job. No signs of breaking and entering, everything thrown around in a mess, only a diamond necklace was missing. Even the 8gig IPod left on the dresser had not been taken. The wife had been out of town visiting her mother, which left the husband. Upon questioning him, the husband became upset at the questioning by Tommy Ray. It was at that moment that everything began to unravel, for the husband and for Tommy Ray.

The husband opened up about his girlfriend, another woman who lived on the same level, just down the hall. They had been seeing each other for almost a year, when he suddenly began having feelings of guilt. Breaking it off was hard, but keeping it secret was harder. He thought that his wife was figuring it out so he decided to buy the necklace. Go figure, using a high-price piece of jewelry to hide months of lying and deceit, it seemed perfect. What could go wrong?

What he didn't know at the time, was that the sales rep he was working with was a friend of his girlfriend's. She told the story, and the girlfriend found an opportunity to make a quick buck. She said she'd come out with the story, or she gets the necklace, but the husband called her bluff. Two weeks later, there was a break-in and no diamond necklace.

Then the phone rang. Tommy Ray let the husband answer it, which of course was a big mistake. It was the wife, who'd been told the entire story by a rather gleeful neighbor. Husband hangs up and doesn't say another word. Then Tommy Ray made another mistake: He left the husband alone and went to speak with the girlfriend.

It took almost ten seconds to determine she was guilty: She opened the door with the necklace on and nothing else, expecting to see an upset ex-boyfriend, which pretty much made it obvious. It was the cursing that made Tommy Ray look back. The boyfriend was running down the hall, calling her every name in his vocabulary. The boyfriend/cheating husband ran down the hall and stopped instantly when he saw the necklace on his now ex-girlfriend. It felt like an eternity in the time it took the man to pull the handgun out from behind him and raise it toward the girl. Tommy Ray stepped in front of him, which of course was the last mistake of the day.

Fifteen days went by before Tommy Ray was emitted from the hospital. By then, the courts had ruled that his job was unsafe to watch over his son, and he'd only gotten visitation rights. Sarah then packed up and moved to Springfield, Missouri with her boyfriend and Tommy Ray's son.

Things could have been worse had it not been for Tommy Ray and his son having always been close. They decided to work it out together and found one temporary option: He bought Daniel a cell phone and paid the bills himself. That way, they could talk every day and not have to hear Sarah complain about the bill. Today was Daniel's basketball game. He wouldn't be home to talk, and Tommy Ray wouldn't be there to watch.

Instead, Tommy Ray sat in his worn-out arm chair, looking out of his third-story apartment window. All he had was a dirty martini and the sounds of the city. Both of which he would soak in several times in the night to drown out the sorrow.

Now, it was morning, and the four Ibuprofen were not kicking in yet. As he dressed, Tommy Ray turned on the television to catch the weather. There was a tall, red-haired, cute weather girl telling him that it was going to be warm and sunny today. But, before she could finish, the background screen changed from a big yellow sun shining over his city, to two hippos in a shallow river, one on top of the other while enjoying themselves. The final caption said, "brought to you by b&j." Tommy Ray silently swore as his cell phone rang; the news station fell into his jurisdiction and this was undoubtedly now his case.

21

"Are you a complete idiot?" Ben screamed. He and Jerry were standing out by the trash can, wasting almost fifteen minutes to take out two bags of trash. The sun was out and only three clouds dared fill the sky. Few cars drove by back behind the building where the trash can was set, The ones that did were usually radio installs, but that happened more on the weekend, not on Wednesdays.

"Dude, it was priceless. Nobody can ever beat that one!" Jerry replied with bits of laughter.

"Why use our names? All it takes is for some cop to connect any one part to us and we're done."

"Don't worry, I'll take it off when I send it to YouTube. Besides, nobody is going to come looking for us based on B & J."

Ben did worry. The last thing he wanted was any kind of attention, especially when they were set to hit the school. Jerry had been fuming so long about the girl, Ben thought hacking the news channel would be a great sidetrack. The problem was that it took almost no time for Jerry to find his way in, and then he screwed it up by putting their names on it. Jerry did make up for it a little with the hippos. Even Ben had to laugh about that.

"Come on, we got to get back to work," Jerry said, trying to get the attention off his mistake. He knew he'd gone a step too far, but nobody had been close to them on any of this, and he was sure he'd covered his tracks.

"Hey Jerry, one more thing," Ben said.

Jerry stopped and looked back at his friend. Ben had gained weight over the last year. Too much fast food, plus he worried way too much about getting caught. "Dude, your killing me with suspense, come on with it."

"Okay." Ben chuckled. "The school is having a Friday morning guest speaker. Some guy from the holocaust is speaking. I think every class is supposed to attend. We could have total access throughout the school." After saying this he looked at Jerry. For the first time in a long time, Jerry looked serious.

"Absolutely," he replied. And with that, the two turned and walked back into the warehouse, both trying to think of ways to take the day off on Friday.

22

The next day began as any other day. Had it not been for the events of the last few days, Calvin would have been bored. First, Becca met him as he stepped out of the shower to discuss her new workout she learned in one of the multitude of magazines she received. Apparently, she could have an hour-glass figure with only 15 minutes of working out a day. Calvin thought to ask her if the fine print stated that one must have the correct DNA to achieve that and not have had kids, but he knew better. Instead, he went straight to the toilet in order to escape the onslaught and capture a few minutes of peace. Outsiders might think that Calvin had a kidney problem if they counted the number of hours he spent in the little room with just a porcelain chair, but Calvin knew better. This was not a place for just depositing, it was also an escape. But instead of taking the hint, Becca continued to talk through the doorway causing the small room Calvin was sitting in to feel more like a padded cell than a small sanctuary.

As Calvin scuffled to the breakfast nook, Maureen began the banging that could wake up Sleeping Beauty on Nyquil. Apparently, Adam made it to the bathroom first today. Calvin had learned to stay out of it. After weeks of losing his voice yelling upstairs, he decided to let it go and see what would happen. Eventually, both kids somehow made it downstairs with all limbs attached and no blood traces to be found. To Calvin, lesson learned: Stay out of it.

As Calvin squeezed behind the wheel of the loan car, he inadvertently looked up into the sky. Calvin peered through the tiny glass windshield looking for something, anything, as if expecting a piano to fall directly on him, a missile to land, or aliens to attack him directly. When little green men failed to appear, and he realized WWIII was not happening, Calvin braced only for the piano which never came. Reluctantly, Calvin started his car and headed for work.

The car picked up speed as he stepped on the gas. It reached nearly 20mph after two minutes. Somehow, after feeling like he was surpassing warp speed, or at least reaching the speed limit, the car was able to slow down at the stop sign. Calvin almost laughed but knew that he would be tempting fate. As he looked each way at his three-way stop, Calvin began subconsciously to turn left to go directly to work the same way he had day in and day out. Fortunately there wasn't anyone at the intersection to see what happened next. Almost in one single moment, Calvin came to and woke from his daily stupor. Instantly, he turned the car around, doing a one-eighty in the middle of the intersection. The car then leapt into motion down the street, going the opposite way from his routine.

It wasn't like Calvin was trying to tempt fate. He just felt that if God was talking to him, he would have to look a little harder. Thoughts of a giant whale coming behind him and swallowing the car whole made Calvin drive just a little faster.

"Jonah, you should have gone to Nineveh," Calvin sang out loud as the Veggie Tales song surfaced in Calvin's mind after years of forced exile.

Calvin's mood brightened the farther he drove away from his work. It built into a joyous laughter as Calvin purposely turned down another road, leading in the direct opposite direction from his job. Now, he was having fun. The thought that no one could find him, even for a little while, was wonderfully pleasing. Another thought entered Calvin's mind: Maybe the Big Man upstairs couldn't find him, either.

On cue, the sirens roared down the hill, flying at Calvin at nearly warp speed. The two police cruisers were coming directly at him. Realizing his tempting fate had caught up with him for reasons unknown, Calvin pulled over and waited to be tarred, feathered, imprisoned, and sent to Davy Jones' locker.

Calvin closed his eyes and waited for the police to begin yelling at him to get out as he pulled over to the curb and put the car in park. Thoughts crossed his mind as the sirens grew loud. What had he done? He had driven a little erratic. Okay. He had demolished a security fence and building and nearly run over a security guard, but he had been trying to help. He had driven away from work. Then the thought hit him: Maybe Candace was using her powers to force the police to track him down and bury him on sight. More thoughts about Candace standing over a kettle of boiling water with a giant mole on her nose almost gave Calvin a chuckle. It was at that moment he realized the sirens were getting quiet as the police cruisers drove past him and farther down the road.

It took Calvin a few minutes to regain his composure and get the nerve to put the car back in drive. As he looked forward he saw that there were two roads he could take, one took a left turn and wound back toward Calvin's job. The other was the road Calvin was currently on and led in the complete opposite direction. Calvin looked each way, then, more determined than ever, decided to keep driving straight. He decided to tempt fate one more time with the most infamous words known to any disaster, "What else could happen?"

As Calvin pulled out onto the street, a black Pontiac Grand Am came from behind him and skidded past him, trying not to collide. No horn acknowledged the mistake, but Calvin imagined the finger he'd be looking at had it not been for Pontiac's dark glass.

Calvin's tiny car lurched forward and followed the path away from work, staying far enough back from the Pontiac that Calvin felt safe. The intersection they were coming to was typical of the city. It had a train track just slightly before the actual intersection. As per Calvin's day, the light on the train track began to go off and the crossing sign arms came down, forcing himself and the happy motorist in the car before him to stop, together.

Calvin stopped almost a full car length back, hoping the distance was enough to ease any tempers that might still be set. He could make out an image of only one person inside and that image didn't seem to move around too much. Then Calvin turned his attention to the train. Somehow, he and the lucky person ahead had the chance to witness the longest, slowest train in American history. Yep, Calvin thought, he could have turned left but tempted fate, instead. Fate scores!

Finally, after miles of seeing the various works of art from a few boisterous boyfriends professing their love a little too much and certain gangs claiming their turf on a moving vehicle that rarely stayed in their turf, the train passed without incident. Calvin almost felt relief that nothing eventful had happened. It was only when the train had passed that Calvin realized the car in front of him had lurched forward, only to stop directly on the train tracks.

Calvin waited, hoping the Pontiac would just pull forward and go away, but nothing happened; the car didn't move. It didn't seem to be running at all. Calvin kept back, waiting, not even remotely daring to use the horn. He just waited for something to happen. It did.

The lights and bells on the tracks began to go off again. Now, Calvin was worried. He pulled his car closer to the car, déjà vu creeping into his mind. He wasn't a kid, and this wasn't his friend, but someone was on the tracks, stuck, and Calvin was the only one there.

SAVE MY PEOPLE.

No. He imagined it that time. He had to have imagined it.

The car stayed there as the arms came down across the tracks. Calvin looked to his right and saw another train coming—and much faster than the last one.

The door to the Pontiac opened and a tall, skinny man got out, whose face seemed to have been weathered by the sun. He left the door wide open and tried pushing the car. The car budged, but only slightly, and then it rested back in its original position, directly on the tracks. He tried again, and the car only rocked slightly.

Calvin looked again at the train coming down the tracks. Against his own better judgment, he found himself getting out of his car and running toward the man. "Get out of the way!" he yelled at the top of his lungs, his words partially drowned out by the train whistle.

The man looked back at Calvin and said something, but between the train and its whistle and his own heart pounding, Calvin couldn't hear anything.

He finally reached the car, his breath coming in spurts as he looked at the man. The man didn't say anything, but just looked at Calvin as if he were a new life form that suddenly appeared before him. Calvin had a choice to make: help or run. He looked down the tracks. The train was now very close, but there was still time. Calvin made up his mind. Crouching down behind the car, Calvin lowered his left shoulder and pushed with all his might. The car began to budge as Calvin looked up. The man was just staring at Calvin.

"For God's sake, push man!" Calvin yelled.

The weathered face acknowledged what was happening and turned to push. This time Calvin put his back to the bumper and pushed again with everything he had. The train let out another whistle and its breaks screeched on the tracks.

For a moment, Calvin thought they were not going to make it when the car lurched. Slowly at first, but with more determination from the men, the more the Pontiac moved.

The car rolled and rolled. Calvin thought that they were in the clear when the car suddenly stopped. Calvin looked back to the car only to see that the back wheels were stuck on the final bar of the track. Without waiting for the man, Calvin bent down again with his back to the car and pushed. Only this time, he lifted the bumper as he did. His muscles burned as his legs cried for a break. The whistle and screech of the train were so loud they vibrated inside Calvin's head. Calvin realized the train was braking and that he had just a slight chance.

That final thought was it. Calvin, teeth clenched and muscles quivering, moved the car past the tracks and a few feet down the road. A swirl of wind engulfed Calvin as he was forced to hold onto the bumper in order to not get dragged into the train as it passed by. The sound of metal-on-metal was everywhere as the train slowed down.

Calvin was tired, out of breath, and every muscle in his body ached, but a little smile began to creep across his face. Feeling a little better about himself and being able to let go of the car as the train slowed down, Calvin turned to talk to the weathered man.

The man had gotten back inside his car again, shut the door, and was trying to start the car. Calvin walked around the car to the driver's door and looked in the window. The man looked very worried and had missed seeing the car's starting problem. Calvin tapped on the window as the man ignored his request and continued frantically to start the car. Again Calvin tapped the window, only a little harder this time. Still the weathered man kept trying.

Finally Calvin knocked hard on the window. The weathered man stopped what he was doing and sat in his seat frozen. He didn't move. He didn't look at Calvin. He didn't even seem to breathe. He just sat there. Finally Calvin tapped again on the glass, startling the man out of his stupor.

The man turned to look at Calvin, as he did so Calvin yelled through the window.

"You have to put the car in park first. Then try starting it."

The weathered man just looked at him as Calvin pointed to the center console where the car was sitting in drive. It took the man a few seconds to look at the gear shift and realize his mistake. Then in a movement that would make a hummingbird look slow, the man slammed the gear shift in park, turned the ignition, threw the car into drive again, and sped off to the intersection and turned right and sped off down the road.

Calvin stood there, stunned for a second, wondering what had just happened. "You're welcome!" was all he could get out.

The train had now fully stopped and he could hear shouting coming from down the train tracks where the engine was. He had had enough excitement for one day. So, Calvin crawled over the connecters of two cars from the train and quickly walked back to his car. With a sigh, he turned the car around and drove back to the street that led to his work.

"Okay, I get it, Jonah, you should have gone to Nineveh," Calvin said to himself as he began to truly laugh for the first time in a long time.

23

Grumpy, that's what he was, just downright old-fashioned grumpy. Tommy Ray was looking to figure out why he was so grumpy, but couldn't put his finger on it.

It wasn't from missing Adam; they'd spoken the night before. They had lost their basketball game; Adam had sat on the bench with four fouls.

"But you should finish the game, you are no use just sitting there," Tommy Ray replied.

"I know, Dad. But coach said it might go into overtime." It didn't, they'd lost by one.

Maybe it was his morning. The day began early with Ms. Rolph's wonderful little dog next door barking and barking and barking. Ms. Rolph was visiting family and a dog-sitter was there to watch the dog during the day, but the sitter didn't come until 8:00 AM. The dog began barking at 4:00 AM.

Next on his agenda was the assignment he'd just been given. It had originally been assigned to Herm, a good detective in Tommy Ray's eyes. Herm had begun the investigation when he got the call that his wife had gone into labor almost five weeks early. Herm wasn't coming back for a few weeks because he had to take care of his wife, so the case was switched over to Tommy Ray. Being a day behind and awake since 4:00 AM, Tommy really wished he'd started drinking coffee about that time.

He tried yoga, which didn't help, and then ran five miles to get his heart going, but still the grumps remained. After a long shower and warm breakfast, Tommy Ray gave in. He was just grumpy and might as well go along with it. Ugh, was all he could say to himself as he walked out the door.

His first stop was at a Quickstop on the outskirts of his jurisdiction. The clerk that had worked that morning was off today and wouldn't be back in until Monday. So Tommy Ray had to talk to Shaeen.

Mistake one was pronouncing the girl's name Shane. He was told it was pronounced Shay-een. Shaeen was a young, slightly overweight girl, standing about five foot two inches and clearly had ancestors from India. She had the attitude of a pit bull as she answered each question as if Tommy Ray had cursed her mom. She spat each answer, but it could have been the gum she was chewing as Shaeen didn't believe in closing her mouth to chew. In order to balance that, she had a nose ring composed of a loop and a stone which appeared to be more of a bugger hanging off her nose than a piece of jewelry. That was balanced out with three loops attached to her right eyebrow and multiple piercings in her ear.

"I told those guys yesterday all about it, didn't they tell you?" Shaeen demanded more than asked.

Tommy Ray didn't have the energy or the desire to go into the explanation about his morning and how he acquired the case. He simply told her he was confirming the statements, which ultimately was the truth in a long-reach sort of way.

"He didn't have a gun or any weapon that I know of," Shaeen said. "He just came in and grabbed a box of Huggies and some hot dogs and a gallon of milk and walked right out the door. Deb's couldn't believe he was doing it until she realized he was driving away."

"So, she didn't confront him in any way?" Tommy Ray asked, assuming Deb was short for Debbie.

"No. She got the car make and called the cops."

"But no license plate."

"No, no license plate was on the car. She said it had a fake tag. Here, look at the video."

Tommy Ray did look and saw a beat up old Pontiac, presumably a Grand Am, driving out of the parking lot. The car had smoked glass so the suspect was more an idea than a fact. But the video had captured a good look from behind the car of a tall man holding the same contents that Shaeen had just mentioned. The car drove left out of the parking lot and disappeared in the distance. Only a few minutes after that two police cars came driving up.

"Guess they got here a little too late, huh?" Shaeen smarted off.

Tommy Ray immediately replied, "Probably would have been here sooner if they were the fashion police." He looked directly at the loops on Shaeen's eyebrow. Then he left the store and got into his car. He had another video to look at with a familiar looking man as the main character.

24

Janiyah's day had begun like the last few days. It had been a rough start. Jessica had been a little help, but the two couldn't be together all the time. It wasn't the classes so much, as the teachers had pretty good control over what was being said, but the passing periods were much different. The hallways parted as she walked down them. Janiyah wasn't sure if it was intentional or just something she was reading too much into.

The stares had picked up considerably as word spread out about who she was and what had happened. Even the comments had picked up, some better than the others.

Has she met Jesus?

Can the voices predict the lottery?

I think she has something metal in her head. Maybe it picks up radio waves!

During second period announcements, the school was notified that a speaker from the Holocaust would be coming by to speak with them in an assembly. His name was Mike James; he had changed his name upon arriving in America. He came every year to tell his story about his survival through Auschwitz and Poland.

Janiyah enjoyed his presentation even though he was rather hard to understand with such a thick Polish accent. Still, she thought, the assembly was fun and nothing bad could happen at an assembly.

25

The research was the hardest part. Neither of them particularly cared for it, but they both knew it had to be done. They staggered their time in and out of work so that one of them could follow her to and from school. They had already tapped into her network at home in order to get onto her computer. But, they needed to see live action, check out her friends, and really just wanted a clear picture of her.

The computer was the easy part. They had long confiscated those "broken parts" from work. Apparently, this girl and her parents hadn't figured out that they needed a password on their computer's wireless router. Both Ben and Jerry knew that any person sitting in the street can hack into another computer that uses a wireless router if a password is not set up. Many people were either not aware of it or too lazy to set it up. This helped as the two simply pulled in front of the house, figured out which line was hers and logged in. Once in, they could see what she was looking at and could even look through her computer when she wasn't home, assuming it was on.

They followed her home and to school when they could. They were even able to sit in the car across the street from the campus and watch her eat lunch outside. Every time they followed her it was the same thing. She sat with one girl whom she got along with very well. Occasionally, another girl or two would join them, but only at the request of the friend.

"So, we have only one girl to really dodge, if we can get her alone," Jerry said later that night as they went over their plan. "How are you doing with that janitor suit?"

"Fine. They changed the patch from last year but it'll still work," Ben replied, looking down at a worn-out blue shirt he'd picked up from the back of a maintenance vehicle several years ago. The patch on the left pocket was faded and the edges were frayed slightly, but it was still intact. The school district had changed patches over the summer, but not every janitor had purchased the new shirts yet.

"Tomorrow," Jerry said more to himself than to Ben.

"Tomorrow," Ben said, affirming their decision. "Tomorrow she gets round two." The rest of the evening was mostly silent as the two simply studied the map on how to get around the gymnasium and to the girls' bathroom.

26

"There, right there, did you see that?"

It did not seem like Tommy Ray and the city worker were looking at the same video. It was nice of him to work quickly to pull up the video from the stoplight, but Tommy Ray would rather have looked at it alone. Well, at least the man didn't have a nose ring.

"He just got into his car and took off, leaving his friend to fend for himself. What a crappy partner," the worker said.

"You're assuming they're partners, then?" Tommy Ray asked in amusement.

"Of course they are. Look at them work together to move the car with all that stolen loot."

Tommy Ray hadn't told the city worker, Mitch, more than he needed to know. Just that a man had made a burglary and driven down this road. He hadn't realized another person had gotten involved.

"Let's see that again, the part on the tracks."

The video showed a man just out of focus trying to move his car off the tracks. Behind him was another man who seemed reluctant to move. The man in the back looked sideways, presumably at the train barreling down and looked back at the man on the tracks. There were several headshakes before the man finally acted.

"He runs to the car and damn near lifts it off the tracks. He must be desperate to save the loot?"

Tommy Ray ignored that last statement. The fact that a train was charging forward was enough. What caught Tommy Rays eye even more was the figure. The camera was used to catch speeders and people running red lights as it sat on top of the stoplight at the intersection just yards away from the railroad tracks. The camera's main use was to catch drivers directly in the intersection and take clear pictures of them and their license plates. The train tracks were too distant to get a clear look at people's faces, but gave enough of an image that you could make out certain details. The detail Tommy Ray was looking at was becoming more familiar.

"Does this zoom at all?" Tommy Ray asked.

"Not without it getting blurry, but I can try," the city worker replied as he clicked on the video with his computer to zoom in closer to the action. As the picture size increased on the screen, the images became slightly more distorted.

"Stop, that's it," Tommy Ray said as he stared unbelieving at the computer screen.

"What do you see?" the city worker asked.

"Someone I need to find," Tommy Ray said.

The city worker burned him a copy of the video and the picture to a DVD and printed a copy of the image Tommy Ray had seen just moments before. When he reached his car and sat down, Tommy Ray pulled out a picture that had been drawn only a few days ago and compared it to the computer image had held in front of him. The image of a man who had completely destroyed three acres of land at IT was now looking directly at him from the side of a train track.

27

Calvin reached work over an hour late, but he didn't care. He walked with a lighter step, his stride just a little longer than it was before. His focus was not on the floor before him; he looked straight ahead, seemingly to search out people who might come across his path. After several hey's, hello's, and what's ups, Calvin reached the pinnacle of path destroyers, Candace.

Coworkers from around the cubicles had been waiting for this moment. It was as if they knew a car was about to purposely back end another car and they couldn't take their eyes off the carnal knowledge. The combustibility of the storm was about to hit full on with an open target, it was must-see TV, if it had been on TV. As Calvin turned the corner and approached Candace, their collective breath inhaled and froze as if one tiny atom escaping their mouths might overpower the foreplay that was happening in front of them. It also added that Calvin was looking directly at the storm, a huge no-no for anyone in the remotest sense of trouble.

Calvin walked directly up to Candace, smiled a wide toothy, but apparently genuine smile. "Hey, Candace," was all he said as he walked past her and on to his cubicle. A collective gasp was heard. Each person looked at each other and then back to Candace and then back to each other. None of them could explain what had just happened. The storm had just been hit by a smile?

Candace stood there, frozen, watching Calvin walk past her and turn the corner to his cubicle. She wasn't sure what had just happened; only that Calvin was not acting like Calvin. As she turned her head back she noticed that the employees were all looking at her. She had to do something, even if it was the wrong thing. She was the boss and they had to know it.

"Calvin!" she shouted as another collective gasp was heard around the office. She felt her composure building and her agitation with this situation taking control. She marched down the maze of cubicles and turned the corner to face Calvin, who had stopped and waited for her. He had actually stopped and waited, instead of scurrying to his cubicle. As she approached, Calvin's coworkers had scrambled into each other's cubicle to get a better look or to hear what was about to happen. The Super Bowl, Academy Awards, or American Idol had nothing on this.

Candace approached Calvin with all the force of a Mack truck in fifth gear. Her sole purpose was to run over and destroy the mark, regardless of who he was and why he was late. What was up indeed?

"Calvin, you are late. Very late," the Mack truck bellowed as she approached Calvin and stood not more than two feet in front of him. Even though she was shorter than most men, Candace found that by standing close to them when they were talking made them uncomfortable and gave her an edge. She did so now. The problem was Calvin neither backed up nor looked nervous. On the contrary, he seemed to be fine with it.

"Yeah, thanks for noticing, Candace," he said with an honest air to it. "I got tied up helping a guy move his car. Well, I got to call Memphis, we'll talk later," was all he said.

He turned and walked away, leaving Candace frozen in place for the second time in less than a minute. All around her people were scurrying to get out of the path of destruction that might come. The Mack truck had been shut down and brought to a standstill, but you didn't want that truck to start up again and aim for you.

Candace, more out of shock than anything else, simply turned and walked back to her office. Behind her she heard what sounded like Calvin laughing, seriously laughing, as she closed the door to her office. She had a phone call to make. Everything could wait; it was all about Calvin now.

28

"Are you freaking crazy?" Gary asked Calvin as they sat together in Calvin's cubicle. Gary sat on top of the filing cabinet next to Calvin, who sat on his chair turned toward Gary. There wasn't much room in the tiny square space so they were almost on top of each other.

Gary had come in almost immediately after the storm had left the area. Everyone else was too afraid to be seen with Calvin in case a Candace sighting suddenly happened. Gary, who usually spent a lot of time with Calvin, could get away with it. Now, he was spending much of the time rambling on and on about what had just happened.

"Seriously, are you crazy?" Gary continued. "Right now Candace is in her office planning on how she can tear you limb from limb."

"Oh, it'll be all right," Calvin replied, although in truth he wasn't quite as confident. It wasn't commonplace to blow off Candace like he did, but he just simply wasn't in the mood to discuss why he was late. The entire episode had flashed before his eyes several times, each of which added to the newfound composure Calvin was showing now. It wasn't ego, Calvin thought, it was composure. He had handled himself in a crisis and survived. Thinking about his failure many years ago on a similar train track cooled his triumph.

"'Yeah, thanks for noticing,'" Gary kept on. "Seriously." With that both Calvin and Gary had to laugh. Calvin hadn't been thinking about Candace, so he just answered off the top of his head.

"I guess I was a little preoccupied," Calvin replied.

"With what? What is this about a car and a train track?"

"Oh, nothing. Just helped a guy move his car, no big deal."

Gary looked at his watch. "Okay, I have a conference call I have to be on. You might think about using the back exit for the rest of the day."

"Thanks." Calvin got out between chuckles. Calvin really wasn't worried about Candace, which was surprising to him. Normally, he would be all upset as he paced back and forth, waiting for the next lightning bolt to strike. Not this time. Now, he felt relaxed.

"Whatever happens happens, I guess," he said to himself as he turned his chair back to his desk and decided he really should call Memphis.

Meanwhile, Candace was fuming. She wasn't exactly sure how to approach the phone call, but knew it had to be made. What she was going to say wasn't clear to her. Her boss, Michael Strain, had made it perfectly clear three months ago. Sales were down and her butt was on the line.

Her problem now included Calvin, one of the top sales reps in the company's history, was showing signs of rebellion. Candace thought she knew why and decided to suck in her ego and make the call. Better to get it out of the way than let it simmer.

She called Martin's office, only to be put on hold by his annoying assistant who seemingly didn't realize the gravity of the situation. Candace had to listen to a couple of minutes of Motley Crue's "Home Sweet Home" played in easy-listening elevator format. Had it not been for the seriousness of the situation, Candace would have laughed. A couple of decades before, she was screaming at the top of her lungs for Niki Sixx to even look at her. She had taken off every ounce of clothing just to get his attention at the concert, which pretty much matched half the girls in the front ten rows. She couldn't get enough of their music. Now, it was on in every elevator in the building, but played with flutes, clarinets, and violins. What had happened? Before she could take the time to picture herself in the black leather skirt and cheetah halter top with mesh leggings, high heels with hair and makeup to match, Martin picked up the line.

"This is Martin," he answered as if she didn't know who she was calling.

"We have a problem."

"What problem."

"Calvin James. I think he found another job." Candace waited for the reaction. Initially, all she got was Martin blowing out air as if his entire existence had completely deflated. Candace knew he was full of hot air, but really.

"Then we have to act fast. What can we do?"

"I know what to do, but it's going to hurt," Candace replied.

"Tell me." And with that, Candace explained her situation and what her plan was. It was hard to hold her ego in, but she knew her job, reputation, and lifestyle hung in the balance on this conversation. She also knew she was making the right decision, no matter what happened from here on out.

"Are you sure?" was all Martin asked.

"Yes. And we should move quickly."

"Then do it. Today." And with that, Martin hung up the phone.

Candace was on her own now, but she had a plan and it was centered on Calvin James.

29

If it wasn't the worst thing that could happen, it was sure close. Janiyah sat in the principal's office, not because she was in trouble, but to keep her out of it. Janiyah sat and looked at a picture of Principal Jones playing golf on some golf course that sat on the ocean. She had never been interested in golf, much less followed it. Green grass, tall trees, white sand in certain areas, and then the bluest ocean crashing into rocks just below where two men stood playing golf. One person was Mr. Lace; she had no idea who the other was. It looked incredible and inviting and Janiyah wished she were there.

Really, she wished she was anywhere but here.

The morning had continued in pretty much the same fashion as it had started. A few whispers, a few stares, ahhh, popularity. Once second period had let out, it was time for lunch. Janiyah had headed for the cafeteria but Principal Jones cut her off. He wanted a few words with her in private and was trying to quickly usher her through the maze of teenagers when Janiyah spotted it. It actually took her a second look before she realized what she was looking at.

School hallways are one of the most unorganized places on earth. There are supposedly thousands of volumes written for rules that the IRS should follow and even these would fail in comparison to the volumes needed to understand teenagers in school hallways. It was chaotic, and this was a good day. The flow was so congested actually people could only move at a foot a minute. It did help to be led by a principal. One of the big rules was to get out of the principal's way. You didn't want them noticing you for any reason, especially if you'd done something remotely incriminating, which was more the case than not.

The people parted as Mr. Jones walked with Janiyah in tow. As they neared the locker area which ran in front of the principals' offices, the sea of hormones pretending to be teenagers spread apart. Janiyah should have realized how serious this was when they passed two people making out, really making out. Mr. Jones didn't even say a word. He just kept on walking, almost pulling Janiyah with him. As they reached the locker area and worked through it, she saw it. On the floor was the school newspaper. Something made her look twice at the paper. There it was plain as day: Janiyah was looking at a picture of herself, the words CRAZY GIRL were captioned just above it and RETURNS TO SCHOOL below it.

Janiyah almost fainted, but Mr. Jones had such a rush going and a tight pull on her arm that she wasn't afforded the chance. In what seemed like a whirlwind, Janiyah was swept through the final locker area, into the reception room, and into Mr. Jones' office. Mr.

Jones then sat her down, told her to stay here while he checked on the situation and said he would be right back. After eons passed, looking at and wishing she could be on that golf course, Mr. Jones returned.

"Janiyah, I am so sorry about this."

"Who printed that story?"

"Well, I'm not quite sure. The writer is said to be I.P. Mayo, but we know that's a joke. Mrs. Sparks, who's in charge of the paper said she hadn't approved it and it hadn't been in yesterday's check. Once it was sent to be printed, it was changed as you see it now. She did mention that she did not check it before the last save, but had approved it several hours before actually sending it to the printer."

"What does that mean, exactly?"

"It means that we believe someone hacked into our computer system and added that article prior to us sending it to print."

Mr. Jones' secretary entered after she'd knocked on the door. She told him some parents for "the other situation" were here and were waiting for him in the conference room.

"Janiyah," he said. "I am sorry, but I need to meet with them. We are trying to get hold of all the papers and shred them. In the meantime, we've called your parents and they are on their way here to get you."

"Thank you," was all she could squeak out.

"I know you're going through a lot right now, but your counselor is always available to talk, if you need her." With that, Mr. Jones walked out of the office, closing the door behind him.

Janiyah and the golf course were alone again.

"I will not go to a counselor, not again," Janiyah said to the ocean as it hit the giant rocks.

"Not again."

30

They were rolling in the conference room. Normally Ben hated it when Jerry did things like this. It was the spur of the moment stuff that led to getting caught. But this time, Ben overlooked it. This time it was worth it.

"Okay, tell me again how you did it," Ben said.

Jerry was glowing from his success. He had the idea when they realized the guest speaker was coming to the high school, so he just wanted to get the ball rolling. He did so in the only manner he could think of, mass publicity.

"You remember that I was on the school newspaper, don't you?"

Ben remembered. Jerry had been harassed for days about that. Right up until Ben and all the other guys realized why Jerry was doing it. One, he was the technology guru for the paper. Everything went though him to be printed, which gave him all the access he needed. Two was Sarah Preston. She was probably the hottest girl in eleventh grade. Now the two of them were working together. It also helped that she believed in loose fitting shirts which tended to hang down when she bent over. It was good to be an overly hormonal teenager. Thank God the pimples kept you humble.

"Yeah, I remember."

"So, when I was there, they asked me to set up everything. I had the stories to set in one spot, the pictures to crop, align, and clean up, and then I had to add graphics to almost anything. The only way to do it was to give me the passwords because Ole Sparks couldn't do it. She didn't have a clue."

Ben had been wondering why he never acted on it before. When asked, Jerry told him it was because he would have been caught. Now, nobody could trace it back to him.

As they both looked down at the school newspaper of the girl that they were about to really toy with, both Ben and Jerry began laughing even harder.

"Dude, we are so going to get her," Jerry said.

"Again," said Ben. His thoughts drifted back to the first time he and Jerry had encountered the girl. What a pain she had become.

Jerry had been working there for almost six months to Ben's year when they had begun their plan to alleviate the store of its "defective" merchandise. They had reigned supreme for three months. Both had upgraded their computer systems part by part. Jerry then focused on games by snagging an Xbox 360. He'd added around 30 games to his stash. Ben had focused more on practical upgrades. He started by gaining a new phone and DVD player. He then "received" his first microwave. And finally, he made the supreme steal of a lifetime with a 40-inch flat-screen TV. Working for a year without incident had paid off in trust from the store manager in letting Ben close the store, which had been all important in their scheme.

It was a busy Sunday afternoon in February when it happened; normally the store was moderately quiet. But, the Super Bowl had come and gone and taken football season with it. Now the store was rustling with men making up their lost time by upgrading their systems in time for the upcoming draft and next year's football season. Ben had heard way too many stories from customers that had gone over to a friend's house who had a killer system. These men had to get that or something just a little better than what their buddy had. This was good for the store and good for bonus checks, but it also meant more work for Ben and Jerry, which neither really wanted.

By late afternoon, the store looked as if the Tasmanian Devil himself had waltzed through each aisle. The employees were exhausted and Ben and Jerry were ready to leave. That was when that girl showed up. She came, with her mom, to return a Sharp DVD player she had received as a gift. Unfortunately for her, Jerry was covering customer service when she arrived.

Jerry knew what the problem was immediately; it was a common problem that most customers were never made aware of. The cables connecting the DVD player to the television were faulty. The male connector for the right audio feed was too short and wouldn't connect in many cases. This gave a distorted sound to the video. It was a simple fix that Sharp had already prepared for. All stores that carried Sharp electronics were given new cables to replace the old ones with. The problem that followed was not the cables, though; it was that Jerry needed a new DVD player.

The return was as normal as any return could go. Jerry exchanged the player for a competing one of similar price and quality. The girl was happy and left the store; Jerry took the player to the back. Later in the evening, before closing, Jerry volunteered to take out the trash. He left the DVD player behind the dumpster wrapped in newspapers. After the store closed, he'd pull behind and pick up his free player. To cover his tracks, the box the player had come in had been taped up with another player that had been in the "broken and not able to repair" stock. It had all worked out until she came back.

With less than fifteen minutes left before the store closed, she came back. She had left a DVD in the player, Pride and Prejudice or some lame girl movie that Jerry could care less about. She needed it back to return to the movie store. To add to the problem, Jerry wasn't covering the return section now, Todd was covering it. Jerry was made aware of the problem when Todd and Ted, the store manager, had called him over asking where the returned player was.

The only thing that saved Jerry that day was Ben. Upon seeing the situation and the old DVD player in the new box and seeing Jerry squirm as he tried desperately to come up with an excuse, Ben went into action. He knew the spot stashed their loot and went there immediately. He found the DVD player, brought it in through the back door and stashed it in the broken stock. He then put on his most absent-minded looking face and walked into the action at the return desk.

"Where is the DVD player now? That's all I want to know," Ted was asking, his forehead creasing with frustration. The girl in front of the counter was looking upset, too, and Jerry was beginning to sweat. Ben moved in quick.

"Hey, are you looking for that DVD player?" Ben piped in.

Ted turned to look at Ben as if he had just asked the most obvious question in the world. He could have asked, "Hey, do you like breathing?" or "Hey, isn't Angelina Jolie hot?" But no, Ben had gone with the DVD question. Just call him Mr. Timing.

"Yeah," Mr. Timing continued. "I put it in the not-able-to-repair stock by mistake. I forgot about those stupid cables."

For a moment, everyone went quiet as if they weren't sure exactly what was happening. The girl spoke up next.

"Can I just get my DVD out of it, please?"

Together, the group moved to the back and retrieved the DVD from the player. Ted watched as he held onto the box with the wrong player in it as Ben plugged in the Sharp player and retrieved the DVD.

"Then explain to me how/why this went player went into this box, Ben," Ted asked. He was pretty agitated by this point. Now it was Jerry's turn to help his buddy out.

"I was in a rush to cover returns and the floor. I must have put the wrong one in the box. I don't know how, but man, that's a big mess up," Jerry said with the best smile he could force.

In the end, the girl got her DVD back, and Jerry was written up for marking the wrong box. Ben was let go with just a verbal mark to check things better before sticking them in the broken stock. Ted, however, was reprimanded by his superiors for allowing this to go on. He was forced to put an internal monitoring system in to video the warehouse. He also began splitting up Jerry and Ben on their work schedules per his superior's orders, just to see if the "losses" would stop. It would not be for another four months until a new manager took over the store, that Jerry and Ben would work together again and renew their crime spree

Jerry never forgot the girl, or the incident. Regardless of whose fault it was, Jerry blamed her. Ben began to see things Jerry's way and followed along. The two then came up with the idea of taking their pranks to another level and direct it toward someone. After hearing about similar stories and pranks in an obscure little book they'd found in a Half Price Books store, they knew exactly who they were getting first.

Now, she was out and free, but the boys still had not forgotten nor forgiven. It was time to get the girl.

31

Tommy Ray had played the video for his boss, and Sergeant Miles Jones had brought in a few others to watch as well, so there was a gathering around the television monitor. After watching the video several times and having every person watching voice a different opinion, the crowd continued to grow. There was such a crowd now that Tommy Ray had to hold his position in front of the monitor just to be able to see it without getting pushed aside. After the tenth viewing of it, Tommy Ray decided to move out of the way and let the others have it. He stood to the side and listened to what they had to say.

"He left his buddy just standing there," Gary Smith said. He had been working traffic lately because he had been written up by internal affairs for illegally breaking and entering a suspect's house to look for evidence. The fact he found ten bags of dope lying on the couch had absolutely no help in his defense.

"There's no way. They aren't working together. They barely address each other." This time it was Detective John Kosh.

Tommy Ray liked him, and better yet, he liked his instincts. John was the kind of detective you saw coming a mile away. He always had on a sport coat, usually brown. He had pants that you could buy from Wal-Mart with matching shoes that always squeaked when he walked on tile. His ties were from the 'eighties, and usually striped. But it was his mustache that Tommy Ray liked the most. It grew thick and covered his upper lip so you couldn't see the lip move, but the outside of the mustache was groomed so that it curled up and pointed back toward his nose. Tommy Ray could never grow a mustache, so he lived vicariously through John's.

"Exactly," Sergeant Miles said. "He nearly gets run down by the train when the other guy takes off. With all that, he never once chases the car or even seems to yell at it."

"Maybe there is more back in his car," another officer suggested.

Tommy Ray didn't know him. He was young and thin and had that look that said he was new. It was the look of youth and energy, before he gets piled on with too many cases.

He continued. "You see how he rushes back to his car and goes the other way. Maybe there was something in the car that made him want to leave."

"Or maybe there is a big ass train parked right in front of him," Detective Kosh replied, sparking laughter all around him.

Even the new guy laughed a little, but he wasn't done with his oracle. "Then why doesn't he wait for the train to move again? He just takes off past the same street he chose not to turn on a few minutes before." With no reply from anybody else, the new guys smiled as if he had just solved the case.

Tommy Ray spoke up. "The suspect is also the same person who tore up the IT grounds a couple of days ago."

Sergeant Miles asked. "Are you sure? The same guy?"

Tommy Ray walked over and tapped the picture of the drawing from the IT fiasco on the left side of the television, and the blown-up picture of the man from the train on the right. The They all saw that they were looking at identical men.

A collective sigh erupted from the group.

"Sure looks like the same guy to me," Detective Kosh said as the others humphed and nodded their agreement. Most had remained quiet during these exchanges. For a moment, the others just looked at the drawing, then the picture and then back to the video.

Finally, Gary Smith broke the silence. "So, what kind of guy tears up a corporation's field and then lifts a car off a train track?"

"You see," the young officer said, "he's trouble."

"He also saved two men's lives at IT and probably that idiot's life on the train track," Tommy Ray added.

All the men turned back to look at Tommy Ray, almost pleading for him to continue.

"So, we either have a renegade with no regard for himself or personal property or we have a man pretending to be a hero and royally screwing it up."

"Or," Detective Kosh added, "maybe a little bit of both."

"All in all," Sergeant Miles added, "he needs to be found and fast before all of this gets worse."

The group dispensed, leaving Tommy Ray and the two pictures of some man in front of him. As Tommy Ray looked at the drawing and then back to the picture and then to the screen, all he could think of was one thing: "Who are you?" He had to find this man, but how?

32

Walking into Candace's office was much like talking openly about feminine products. For a man, it was beyond painful. Calvin had just been called by Candace to come in and speak with her. Normally she would announce this over the intercom and demand his presence while she allowed the words to sink in to all listeners. But this time, she had called him on the phone and asked him to come speak with her.

As Calvin made the trek to the office, he decided to keep a positive mind about the situation. So, he had been late, mouthed off to his superior, and had been acting almost completely irrational. What did he have to fear? He began to laugh quietly at his situation. He could almost hear the faint yell from over his right shoulder: someone had said, "Dead Man Walking" as Calvin walked towards the pit of doom.

Once he reached the door, Calvin gave what he assumed would be one last look at what had been his home-away-from-home for many years. It had been a great job and he had made plenty of friends. Even still, nobody raised their face to greet him. They all knew what was coming and didn't want to take a chance that they might go down with him. The Titanic was sinking, better to look the other way than get caught in the downdraft.

Calvin turned to the office, took a deep breath, put on his "happy face" and opened the door. "What's up, Candace?" Calvin almost couldn't believe his own casualness. Did he really sound this cool?

Candace had a look on her face that Calvin had not seen before. Her eyes met his, but glanced away after just a moment. "Thanks for meeting with me, Calvin. Here, have a seat," she motioned as she moved around her desk to sit in the chair next to his. Both chairs had been positioned so they faced each other slightly, but still opened to the desk. Calvin had to sit and turn his neck to his left side just to see Candace. It hurt to twist his neck and the moment felt so important that he decided to turn his chair and face her straight on. He picked the chair up with a lunge, bent forward a bit, and forced the chair to rotate right. With a great plop, the chair thundered as it landed. He quietly pushed aside the thought of how his back would be feeling in the morning.

Calvin faced Candace, who looked shocked at this latest development. Then, with a sigh she tried to hide, she mimicked the action so she could face Calvin directly.

Now sitting and looking at each other eye-to-eye, Candace seemed tiny for the first time to Calvin. She had a look that he hadn't seen from her before, and wasn't sure what to make of it. Her look almost made him pity her. He decided he had to help her and get this out and over with.

"Candace," Calvin began as his voice began to break up, "let's get this out in the open and just say it."

"Well, I do have a few things to say," Candace began with almost a whisper. The look became sadder as she tried to force the words.

Calvin had had enough. If he had learned anything through the last couple of days it was that things were better when faced head on. His middle school football coach used to say, "You can't make milk by staring at the cow." Calvin almost rolled his eyes at the cheesy sports metaphor. "I have plenty of contacts in this business. I will be just fine. So, just go ahead and say it and let's do this." Sweat formulated on his skin, but Calvin refused to wipe it or even acknowledge it. Did he just say he would be fine?

Candace was frozen. Her mouth was slightly ajar and her face must have had a strange look on it as Calvin gave an astonished look at her. Upon seeing this, Candace forced herself to transform back into the same strong woman Calvin was used to seeing. "Don't be silly. We are the fastest growing company in baby foods and you are a huge reason why. I know you have other opportunities, but this is your home."

This time it was Calvin's turn to be stunned. What was Candace actually saying? Was she really not firing him?

She continued. "All I want to know is what they are offering you. No, scratch that," she said.

Calvin joined the mouth-ajar club, but quickly shut it. He was trying to understand what was happening, but the thoughts were too absurd. Who was offering what? Calvin let out his breath so fast it almost sounded like a grunt.

Candace, of course, noticed this and began to panic. She wanted this to go so much better than it was, but her composure was failing. This man was laughing at her. She decided to be quick and direct. At least it would get over with sooner this way.

"I have spoken with the Board. We want to offer you the Director of Sales position. As you know, I've been doing both it as well as my job and it has grown too big for me to handle."

Calvin wasn't sure, but he thought Candace was making part of this up. It didn't matter; he didn't know what to say. The same ol' grunt came out of his mouth once again.

She continued. "The job will have all the regional sales managers' report to you and you will be able to personally hire someone to take your spot. In addition, you will receive the same percentage of sales you receive

A Voice from the Restroom

now for your bonus, but it will be based on total sales, not regional."

Calvin thought he'd just wet himself. Candace wasn't firing him, she was promoting him. For a second, he thought maybe he should just grunt since it seemed to be working so far. The problem was his stomach was churning so hard, he was afraid the grunt might turn into a full-force belch. A promotion and a raise, wow. He just sat there in silence unsure of how to continue.

Candace, though, was completely beside herself. This man was not talking nor was he agreeing. She had thrown a very good, yet painful offer on the table. Giving up control of sales was not something she wanted to do, but this request had been pressured on Candace privately by higher ups. This was now her responsibility to complete.

"This is a good offer. It comes with control over sales, personnel, and even a front parking spot," as if that final part was the cherry on the whip cream.

"I don't know what to say," Calvin squeaked out. Sweat was soaking into his clothes. Calvin quietly thanked God for antiperspirant.

"Say yes," Candace implored and held out her hand.

Calvin reached out and shook her hand and nodded.

Candace gave his hand a squeeze and then released it quickly. "We will get your cubicle moved into your new office today. So, take some time and get your ideas together. You'll report to Chad Taylor, VP of Sales, tomorrow."

Calvin stopped short of running out of the office and looked at Candace once again. The idea of what she just said had not formed in Calvin yet and he let the words soak into him faster than the sweat could pour out. "You mean I won't be working for you anymore," the you sounding a little too harsh, but Calvin went with it anyway.

Candace gave him that I'm-laughing-but-really-thinking-about-pulling-your-eyes-out laugh. "Of course not. We are now both directors! We just have to find a way to work together to make this work. You report to Sales and I to Operations." Candace put on the smile of a lifetime and Calvin appreciated her effort. Candace directed Calvin up and out of his seat and toward the door. Again she forced a smile across her face. "Welcome aboard. Just go home and have a nice day with your family and we will get you moved in."

Calvin had no more than stepped out of the door than it slammed right behind him. Again, no looks up from the desks. Finally, Gary came running up and followed Calvin toward the exit.

"So, what kind of package did you get? They're gonna give you at least medical for six months while you look for a new job, right?" Gary asked, pouting a little as he asked it.

Calvin stopped and looked at Gary. A smile spread across his face. "She made me Director of Sales. I start tomorrow." He turned and walked out, leaving Gary frozen in his tracts with his mouth wide open.

Candace walked back to her desk and sat down. It took her a few minutes to compose herself before she picked up the phone and dialed.

"Well?"

"It's done. He's in."

33

Calvin drove to the church, still wanting a few answers. His questions were beginning to pile up with no sign of any answers coming. The sign still invited anyone to come in and speak and Calvin still had the same feeling: pure, unequivocal fear. Only this time it was joined with something else. Maybe a sense of need for the truth or maybe a desire to find answers or maybe it was just the day he was having. Regardless, Calvin opening his car door, got out, and walked to the church.

It seemed the closer he got, the more his stomach churned inside him. As he reached for the door, his stomach leapt and did a triple somersault with two-and-a-half twists, with a degree of difficulty 3.5. When he opened the door, a cool breeze engulfed him, bringing a smell of vanilla with it from lighted candles which sat on top of tables in the corridor that led to the sanctuary.

Rows of pews stood on the left and right side of an open aisle that led directly to a cross covering an entire wall with Jesus hanging from it, a thorn crown, and blood, and a tiny cloth along his mid-section all that adorned the statue. Below that was an area for a choir. A table and a pulpit stood in front of that, with the pulpit set off just a little to the left. A rail ran along the front of all of it with cushions on the floor before it.

There were windows that ran along the back wall and in three-foot sections along the wall to the left. Each window was vibrant with color from multiple stained-glass windows. The right held no windows, but had another door that led to a hallway. Farther up were three tall wooden boxes that Calvin almost mistook for coffins before realizing they were there for confessionals. There were no visitors in the sanctuary but there was one man walking around in a brown robe dusting the hand rail in front.

Calvin walked to the third pew from the front and sat down as close to the aisle as he could get. After sitting down for a few minutes and looking around at the glass windows for a fifth time, Calvin realized he had no idea what to do. "Okay, now what?" he murmured to himself.

"Pardon me. Were you talking to me?" the man who was doing the cleaning asked.

"Uh, no, but I guess you could help me. I mean, I know you can help me, but, well, I, you see, the sign out there, well . . ." Calvin pleaded with his eyes as he stumbled over the right words to use.

The man cleaning the rail smiled and nodded. "Would you like to speak with the priest?" With a nod from Calvin, he continued. "I will be glad to get him for you. He just went to make a phone call. I'll tell him you're waiting." Then the man began to pass Calvin before he stopped directly in front of him and turned to look Calvin in the eyes. "Will you want a confessional or a private conversation?" He whispered even though there was nobody around to hear the conversation.

The thought of sitting inside the wooden boxes with a faceless priest did not appeal to Calvin in the slightest. Maybe it was the salesman in him, but he liked to do things face-to-face. Talking in a box was like talking on the phone; it served its purpose, but had nothing personal involved with it.

"Private conversation will be fine," Calvin answered as the man swept past him and down the hallway to the right. Calvin sat down in a pew and looked at his surroundings again. He was alone with a twenty-foot Jesus and colored windows; he began to wonder what he was doing here. The events of the last couple of days had been mind-boggling. He had gone from the worst plane ride in his life to a near-death experience with Godzilla and then had nearly killed himself playing chicken with a train before insulting his boss so bad that she gave him a raise. Calvin had to laugh at that, and he began to before being interrupted.

"Well, that's the first time I entered with a chuckle." A man walked up to Calvin and sat down on the pew in front of him. "Charles Garrett," he said as he extended his hand to make a firm handshake with Calvin. "I am the priest here at St. Mary's. Welcome."

Charles Garrett did not dress like a priest in Calvin's mind. Besides being tall, he was well built for a man who appeared to be in his sixties. He had short, thinning gray hair. He wore a blue dress shirt and dark blue jeans. As if understanding what Calvin was looking at, Charles answered him directly.

"I do not care so much for the priestly robes every day. After being here for nearly twenty years, I am afforded a little leeway." Charles grinned. "So, what brings you to the Lord's house?"

Calvin wrestled with the words, trying to force them out. The laugh that had so quickly formed before had disappeared and taken all the moisture from Calvin's mouth with it. All Calvin could usher out was a mild nasal grunt. Calvin James, rhetoric genius.

"You know," Charles said, causing Calvin to jump at the welcomed interruption. "Whether you say it or not, He knows. So, it's easier just to let it out so we can move on in our own lives." Charles reached over and put his arm on Calvin's shoulder. If felt like a weight was being removed as Calvin looked up at the priest.

It was obvious from Calvin's face that he understood. Charles had been in this situation several times and Calvin felt somewhat safe, even though he wasn't quite sure how to say what he had to say. With a deep breath and no direct thought, Calvin just opened up and let it out without one breath.

"When I was a kid, I messed up pretty bad and I know God was trying to help me. So, I lived for many years with that, assuming God had pretty much moved on. But now, something has happened and it seems like God is trying to give me a second chance. The problem is that the priest I spoke to many years ago said there are no second chances. So, basically, I need to know. Am I being tested, are there second chances, or am I just screwed?" Calvin finished and took a deep breath. He felt lighter, freer, somehow just a little better than he had a moment ago. It was out there now. At once, though, he realized he was even more vulnerable than before and quietly pleaded for Charles not to ask him about the voices, Godzilla, and especially the train.

"Well, that's been piling up for awhile, hasn't it?" Charles the Priest, aka Captain Obvious, said. As Calvin's nerves began to gain momentum, Charles continued. "Well, to answer you directly, as I know it, the priest you speak of is right, to a point."

Calvin's heart skipped a beat. What did he just say? Calvin was about to argue and explain that God had just sent a fifty-foot reptile onto the hood of his car and allowed him to live. How about that for a second chance? However, Charles moved to sit down next to Calvin as he continued.

"You see, God lives for us now. A second chance means that we only had one chance to get it right in the first place. Now, seriously, how many times do we ever get it right in the first place?" Charles took a moment to let that sink in, noticing that Calvin's breathing had slowed and he had Calvin's full attention.

"God doesn't count chances. He takes each day as a new day, each chance as one unto itself. To say that God wants you to make up for what happened when you were a kid would mean that he never forgave you in the first place. God forgives easily; we forgive ourselves much less often."

Calvin was now completely numb. His tongue had to weigh near eighty pounds, with no chance for speaking. Instead, he looked at the priest, his eyes pleading for him to continue.

"God may be testing you, or he may simply be helping you. That is something only he knows. What happened before, that is something that you need to deal with. God has already moved on and forgiven. You need to forgive yourself. As for what is going on now, open your heart and see what happens."

As Calvin sat in the tiny car under one single lamp glowing in a parking lot darkened by the night sky, he tried to take in everything that was happening. He had failed as a child to save his friend, but now had saved two other strangers thanks to a voice that may or may not have been God in a restroom in the airport. Oh, he had also destroyed the property of a major corporation, nearly been hit by a train, and had projected his career further in three days than he had in the last three years.

Slowly, he pulled down the visor used to block the sunlight, useless now because of the dark. On the reverse side was a mirror that, when the cover flipped up, brought out a tiny light. Staring in the mirror between the two tiny lights, Calvin could see his face clearly. Then, in one single solitary moment, Calvin summed up all of his life's events culminating in the hard-to-believe acts of the last week with all the poetic oratory skills that he could muster up at one time.

"Wow."

34

It was with the help of modern technology that Tommy Ray was able to track down the beat-up old Pontiac. First, he followed the intersection cameras as he traced the path the car made. It took a while, having to backtrack to look at multiple intersections the car could have traveled down. But, finally, he was able to watch it turn left into an apartment complex.

Next, he pulled up a list of all the renters in the complex. He checked the list to find all the owners of Pontiac Grand Ams. Next, he ruled out anything white or light in color. The video was black and white and had shown a dark-color car, so ruling the lighter cars out was pretty easy. Finally, he was left with three cars to look for. One was a dark green, the other two were black. Fortunately he had one more way of narrowing it down. The car he was looking for had temporary or fake tags.

Tommy Ray pulled into the apartment complex driving his own personal vehicle. The complex was not the worse he had driven through, but it was bad enough. A police vehicle, even an undercover one, would be easy to spot and would cause quite a stir. Tommy Ray wanted to find the car without being spotted first.

The first car he saw was parked out by the pool, or rather algae pond. There was an eerie green on the sides of the pool and throughout the water. One man was working at it half-heartedly as he was talking on his cell phone. The back of his black Pontiac stuck out into the parking lot. The car was parked in a handicap parking space with the trunk wide open. Chlorine powder and pellets were loaded in the back, alongside several buckets and brushes. Also on the back of the car was its license plate. Tommy Ray moved on.

Fortunately, Tommy Ray did not have far to go. A second Pontiac was also in the parking lot and was easy to see. It had taken up two spaces by parking slightly over the white line just enough that no other cars could park alongside. Tommy Ray drove over to the car, got out and walked around it. There, staring right at Tommy Ray was the expired paper license plate in the window. As Tommy Ray peered inside, he noticed the actual license plates lying on the rear floorboard of the car. He returned to his car to call in the numbers.

Tommy Ray sat in his car and took the scene in all at once. It was an old apartment complex, but not a place that housed hoodlums. He had not been called out here before for any problems, which told him that it was a respectable complex, just not an upscale one. It was midday, so there were very few people out and about, which meant many of them were either working or sleeping, which was a good sign for what he had to do. Outside there was little going outside, except for the pool man, who was hardly cleaning the pool. An older, African American woman farther down the parking lot unloaded her groceries from a well kept 1979 Cadillac. He heard the distant sound of an ambulance. All in all, Tommy Ray felt like this would go pretty smooth, right up to the moment that he actually radioed in.

Tommy Ray didn't like or want to have backup. The problem about needing backup was not in capturing the suspect, but having a credible witness support you against outlandish claims. Having another officer on the scene, even patrol officers, kept the outlandish tales of "he didn't read me my rights" or "I was trying to cooperate before he began to beat me for no reason" crap from coming up. As he called it in a familiar voice responded back.

"Tommy Ray, is that you?"

"Hello, Yolanda, how are you and Terrance?" Normally, chit-chat on police radios was unwelcome, at the least. But Yolanda had worked for the city for nearly fifteen years, the last ten in dispatch. It also helped that she had missed only three days in those ten years for being sick and had a work ethic that made even the hardest of workers look like truants. Terrance, her husband, worked in narcotics and had helped Tommy Ray on many occasions.

"He's good and we're good. Is this an emergency?"

"No, just needing some backup."

"Your cruiser shows to be in a parking lot, so where are you?"

"At the Country Hills Apartment complex, just off Spring Valley."

"So tell me, are there any county hills at your complex? Oh, did you hear I am pregnant?" Tommy Ray waited a moment to finish laughing before answering.

"No, no hills, but congratulations. Third one's the charm to get that boy, huh? Yeah, I am at the complex right now, going to apartment two-three-seven."

There was a pause before Yolanda came back, which was not typical for her. "Did you say apartment two-three-seven at the Country Hills complex?" Yolanda replied with her professional voice.

The hairs on the back of Tommy Ray's neck began to stand up. "Yeah, why?"

"Because an ambulance has been called to that very location."

"For what?"

"Apparently, a man in that apartment is having a heart attack."

Without waiting for the backup or even to hear back from Yolanda, Tommy Ray was out of his car, and running full speed towards the stairs that lead him to apartment #237. In the background, Tommy Ray could hear the ambulance's siren grow loud as it turned into the complex's parking lot. Tommy Ray didn't look back, but went straight to the apartment which had its door slightly open. Tommy Ray didn't wait; he just pushed the door open, surveyed the scene and went straight in.

35

They had options. They could conceal a speaker in plenty of places, mainly the ceilings above the bathrooms, or they could use a smaller speaker and put it behind the toilets or possibly the hand towel dispenser. But their favorite choice was a brand new idea and the boys were dying to get to use it. It was the smallest and clearest speaker they had seen, or more conveniently, the best one the store stocked. It just so happened to exist within the new Blackberry smart phone. By dismantling it and taking out the speaker, as well as adapting it to their needs, Ben and Jerry now had a very small, very powerful speaker.

The tiny speaker could pick up and receive voices, but only within short ranges. If they could find a way to place it on the girl, then they could get to her anytime and anywhere given that they were in range. They tried all sorts of sticky substances but finally decided on double sided tape to keep the speaker from standing out too far. If that did not work, they would have to use the distraction of the guest speaker to work the bathrooms by placing speakers in each one.

The plan called for Ben to enter as a janitor, using a uniform the boys had copied easily by watching other janitors walk in and out of the school each day. Jerry had long since taken care of the key issue. Back in his school newspaper days, one janitor had left her keys lying around. Jerry had simply picked them up and run a few "errands" for the paper, which consisted of stopping by the local hardware store and getting a couple extra copies of the key made.

Jerry wouldn't enter the school in fear of being seen. His track record and his face were still too well known, but Ben could blend in.

Ben entered the school as a janitor who'd been sent by Administration due to the illnesses running through the janitorial department. He had purposely grown out what little facial hair he could and had used temporary tanning lotion to make his white face look considerably darker, though nobody questioned having extra janitors around the school. There was always a mess somewhere to clean up.

Ben worked the school by dragging along a trashcan on wheels. The speakers they planned on placing in the bathrooms were set at the bottom of the can with a box over them to protect them. The can was then lined with several trash bags in case anything with fluid was thrown into the can.

Almost immediately upon moving through the halls, Ben was relieved that he had extra lined the can. As the bell rang, signaling that students were to leave their class for the next one, the halls flooded with students going in every direction. As they passed Ben, cans of Monster and Red Bull went flying into the trash can. Occasionally, a diet Pepsi or Fanta would make the grade. Even rarer a bottle of water or juice made the ascent.

Ben moved through the stream of students swimming towards their class with cell phones in hand, talking to someone even though they walked with a friend right next to them. Ben assumed it was okay since those friends were also talking on cell phones. The ones not talking on their phones were either texting someone or making out in the hallways with one hand on their partner and the other holding onto their cell phone.

After trying three different hallways, Ben was able to locate the girl. He'd been worried she'd be hard to find, but as it turned out, it was pretty easy. As the girl walked down the hall, the students parted way as if she had some kind of contagious disease that made getting close to her a bad idea. Ben almost felt sorry for the girl until he remembered what he and Jerry had gone through after they met her. Jerry's voice snapped him out of it. They'd decided not to use walkie-talkies this time since the principals used them at the school now. Instead, Jerry was calling Ben on the cell phone. Ben felt like he was in school again getting to walk down the hall and chat.

"Have you found her yet?"

"Yeah, she's in front of me. Man, nobody is speaking to her."

"Bummer, but who cares? Can you get to her?"

"No. The crowds part when she walks. Nobody wants to get close to her. If I approach her, I'm going to stand out."

"Okay, just stay close and wait for your moment. Do you have it ready?"

Ben looked down into his hand at the tiny little speaker. It had a tiny piece of double-sided tape. One side of the tape had already been attached to the speaker and the other side was ready to be slipped off. As soon as Ben looked up to see where the girl was, he immediately shut the phone off and stuffed it into his pocket. He looked ahead and began to move.

The girl had walked past a group of what appeared to be the popular people. Ben noticed that many of the guys had letter jackets on and the girls had plenty of makeup. He also realized with dismay that big hair was coming back into style. What had prompted Ben to move was the fact that one of the guys in the group had thrown a paper airplane right at the girl and it had landed and stuck in the back of her hair.

Ben rushed to catch up to her as the girl tried to hurry her steps to get away from the crowd while simultaneously trying to pull the plane from the back of her hair. Nobody was helping her, but plenty of people were pointing and laughing. Finally, he caught up to her, and with the word "Miss." He reached out and pulled the plane from her hair. The girl hardly looked back. She glanced back with a forced smile and a quiet "Thanks" and rushed off down the hall and around the corner with the plane out of her hair, but with a tiny little speaker stuck to the back of her collar.

"Jerry," Ben called back on the cell phone.

"Yeah," Jerry replied.

"We're ready."

36

It had been a great morning all things considered. First, Calvin had gotten up before the alarm clock went off. Then, instead of going in to work immediately, he surprised the kids by driving them to school, which was met by the expected pleas from Maureen to drop her off at the corner so her friends would not see her. Still, both Adam and Maureen were pretty surprised to have Dad taking time with them. Calvin made a mental note to do this much more often.

Instead of driving to work, Calvin returned home. Becca had spent the extra time she'd suddenly had sitting on the upright chair in the living room to finish reading her book, *How to Invest in Stocks from Home in only 15 minutes a day*. Calvin had surprised her when he showed up back at the house. Normally, Becca was cleaning, or PTA-ing or some kind of -ing.

"What are you doing home? Aren't you supposed to be going to work?"

Either the words just wouldn't formulate or Calvin didn't really know what to say. His life had been turned upside down in the last few days, most of which Calvin couldn't explain how or why. But right now, Calvin could care less. The one thing he did realize, he had been given a second chance, and with second chances changes had to be made. Especially changes with one's own life.

Without answering her, Calvin walked over to Becca, took the book from her hands and tossed it on the ground. Then, lifting her off the chair, he carried her back to their room and closed the door. He gently laid her on the bed, watching Becca's smile spreading across her face. Then, with a little laugh at himself, Calvin stood back up, walked back to the door of the bedroom and opened it. He turned back to Becca, and with a running start, dove on top of the bed as if he were a teenager again.

After taking the morning with Becca, Calvin then casually drove to work. There were no falling signs, no trains chasing him down, and no cars cutting him off. Indeed, Calvin seemed to actually make most of the green lights today and got to work in less time than usual. He pulled into the parking lot and had driven right past it without seeing it. He had to stop the car, put it in reverse, and back up to see it properly. There, on the front row was an open parking spot. Normally, these spots were all taken, but there was a reason for this one to be open. There on the sign was Calvin's name.

With a smile that had started several hours before and now grew even more than Calvin thought possible, he put the car in drive and slowly pulled into his parking spot.

37

The guest speaker that day was Mike Jacobs. He had the most amazing stories, both sad and full of hope from his experiences in the holocaust. Janiyah had heard him speak once before and was enthralled with the idea of keeping hope alive among the most desperate of any situations. His thick Polish accent was difficult to understand at times, but she had read his book of hope amid the devastation of the holocaust and war torn Europe and could decipher what he was saying.

After his presentation, Janiyah waited for the auditorium to clear out before moving into the line waiting for Mr. Jacobs' autograph. The bell dismissing classes sounded as soon as she stepped in the back of the line. Janiyah didn't mind being late for her next class, it would only mean that less people would be in the hallways to ridicule her. Janiyah stepped up as the line moved and was now only three people away from getting her book signed when the tardy bell for the next class rang. A tiny smile spread across Janiyah's face knowing the freedom she would have in the halls.

After getting her book signed, Janiyah decided to take the long way to class. She had English next and was in no hurry to begin her reading of *1984*. As soon as she left the auditorium, she heard someone call for her. She turned around to look for him, as it was a man's voice echoing in the hallways, but nobody was there.

"Janiyah," the voice came again, but nobody was there. Just then one of the girl's who had been in line with Janiyah getting her book signed, raced back into the hallway and entered fast into the auditorium. Janiyah just stood there for a second not knowing what was going on.

"She can't hear me, Janiyah," the voice echoed again, this time sending chills up her neck. Then the girl exited the auditorium and looked at Janiyah.

"Forgot my backpack," she said as she threw her backpack over her shoulder.

For a moment, Janiyah almost asked if she heard something, but thought of how much torment she'd get in the hallways later if the news of it spread. Instead, Janiyah let the girl move ahead and leave and she headed for the bathroom. She ran into a stall and locked the door, hoping with all her might that nobody watched her enter.

"Janiyah, this is God. Stop running and listen," the voice came again, sounding irritated.

Janiyah dropped to the ground, losing her books. She curled up into a ball and reached to pull her knees to her chest. Janiyah tried with all her might to argue with the voice, but she knew the voice was the same one that she had heard a year ago.

"Janiyah!" the voice bellowed, making Janiyah jump. "Save him, Janiyah."

It took Janiyah a few moments to fully understand what was being said to her. Even then, she truly didn't know what she was supposed to do.

"Save him Janiyah, save him."

"Save who?" Janiyah yelled. Her voice was barely audible through the tears that had begun to flow.

"You'll know. Look for the star."

"Leave me alone, please," she pleaded, now rocking back and forth, holding her knees to her chest. The tears had become a full-force river.

"Look for the star, Janiyah. Now leave."

Janiyah didn't wait. She grabbed her books in one fell swoop and ran out the bathroom door, running straight into a custodian who caught her and kept her from falling. The custodian held her back as Janiyah battled to regain her composure. She did not dare look him in the face. She just wanted to get away. With tears flowing, she turned and ran out the door that led to the student parking lot. Without hesitating, she ran across the parking lot, across the street without looking, and all the way home.

38

Ben had to walk out halfway through the "encounter." Jerry was taking his God approach again and was classic. Finally, he had gathered himself enough to go back to the bathroom. It was his job to walk in and find her. He would then help her out and grab the speaker hidden on her shirt at the same time. As he approached the door, it suddenly flew open and the girl ran into him. Out of instinct, he kept her from falling. It took a second for him to catch his breath before he realized she was running off. Quickly, he reached out and grabbed for her collar. With just the tip of his middle finger reaching it, the speaker got trapped and then hung for a second on her collar.

Ben held his breath for a moment, realizing that it had gotten away and that the girl might find it. But, as she reached the doors to run outside and opened them, the rush of outside air blew into the hallway and with it the speaker sailed off and down to the floor.

Ben picked up the tiny speaker, put it in his pocket, and then went back to the bathroom to help Jerry, who'd been hiding in the ceiling. Both had known that the ceiling in the school was a huge open space that extended throughout the building. As long as you walked only where the walls stood, you'd be fine.

When Ben reached the bathroom, Jerry was just walking out. He was proud of his acting job.

"God again?" Ben asked.

"Yeah, wasn't it awesome? I had to go with it again for her sake."

With a congratulatory high five, the two of them gathered their equipment, placed it into the janitor's push basket that was set just down the hallway out of site. Then they walked out the door Janiyah had run out of and through the parking lot to their car. They didn't speak once about it until they got into the car for fear the girl might still be there or someone would overhear them. It didn't even dawn on them that they had parked in the student parking lot, not the custodial lot.

Once they put the gear away and climbed into the car, Ben and Jerry had a brief moment of silence as they thought about what had just happened. Then, in an instant, they both immediately broke out laughing.

"Dude, that was really awesome," Ben exclaimed.

"Yeah, it was. She willn't bother us again or anybody else for quite a while."

"No, she won't."

"Thanks for replacing the batteries in that piece-of-crap microphone. I guess that was all it needed," Jerry said.

"I didn't replace them; I thought you did," Ben replied as the two of them looked at each other. Then they both began laughing again.

"Wow, I guess it was just meant to be, then," Jerry exclaimed as Ben started the car and drove out of the student parking lot, both laughing at their great accomplishment.

39

When Tommy Ray got to the apartment, he realized the door was open and saw his suspect, Jason Lee, lying on the floor, having a heart attack.

Jason Lee was in his mid- to late-thirties, with rusty red hair, was tall and slightly heavy.

A woman was standing over the suspect, yelling and crying hysterically and a baby was screaming in a bedroom in the back of the apartment. The woman, Hispanic and much shorter than the suspect, was wailing in Spanish and looked completely frightened.

Tommy Ray moved fast to physically escort her to the beat-up old couch that sat along the far wall of the room. He flashed his badge and explained who he was. Not knowing Spanish made things hard, but he tried what he could. First, he looked at her and gave her a quiet sign by placing his finger in front of his mouth. Next, he motioned to her to just breathe, by showing her to take deep breathes.

She showed she understood by answering him in proper English. "I know how to breathe," she said.

Tommy Ray stopped for a moment, nonplussed by the revelation, before she snapped him out of it.

"What about my husband!" she exclaimed.

"You need to calm down," Tommy Ray replied. "The more the excitement, the harder it is for him to stay calm and we need him to be calm." The seriousness in Tommy Ray's eyes was related to the woman who then sat back and closed her mouth.

"The paramedics are almost here. Until then, all we can do is keep him calm. Ma'am, please go help your baby."

With the woman now gone, Tommy Ray was able to direct his attention to the man. The man was trying to say something, and straining to do so.

"Don't talk, Mr. Lee. We have everything in control. Just relax and you'll be fine." Tommy Ray didn't want to bring up why he was really here for fear that the additional strain on his heart would be too much. Tommy Ray called that the "duh" factor. It seemed to work. Jason Lee visibly relaxed as much as he could and just stared up toward the ceiling. There was a knock on the open door with a shout that EMT was here.

After getting Jason Lee down the stairs and into the ambulance, he was taken to Northside Hospital. Tommy Ray waited for the woman and her baby to get dressed before taking them there himself. He thought it was the right thing to do, considering how upset the woman was. Besides that, he had some questions he wanted answers to.

The ride over revealed more to Tommy Ray than he was expecting. The woman's name was Maria. She was half white and half Hispanic. Her father met her mother in Brownsville, TX and married. Maria was born in Texas, giving her full citizenship. She had met Jason Lee while both were working at UPS.

After having their baby, Sarah, Maria had complications healing. She was forced to stay in the hospital for an extra week and return monthly for the doctors to check her healing process. What mattered most was that she could no longer work and their healthcare had been maxed out. Faced with mounting bills and less income, they began selling what they had in order to survive.

"You sold your fridge?" Tommy Ray asked, realizing that he had seen one in the kitchen.

"Yes. We had a very nice refrigerator and sold it to an elderly man down the hall. Then we went to pawn shop and bought a used one. It gave us nearly two hundred dollars!" Maria sounded excited about that despite the situation. It was one of her few bright spots in a long time. "Eventually, we were broke again. His job pays the rent and food, but nothing else. Children need formula and diapers, which is something we can't afford."

"So, Jason Lee found another way of getting them," Tommy Ray finished her statement. Maria's silence confirmed what he said. Tommy Ray had kept driving as Maria looked out of the window. He had long learned as a detective that silence was one of the most powerful weapons you had when questioning someone. People would rather talk than let silence linger. Words gave you comfort that you were in control, even if you weren't. Silence made you feel weak, alone, and that was the last place you wanted to be if you were in trouble.

After a few moments, Maria continued. "He never stole anything we didn't need." Maria hugged her baby tighter as if her presence gave Maria the strength she needed to continue. "He only took food, diapers, and formula and never from the same place twice," Maria added. "You have to understand, it ate him up."

"What did?" Tommy Ray asked.

"Taking that stuff. We needed it; she needs it." Now the tears were in full force. "He hated stealing, but we were going to lose our apartment and we have nowhere to go. I can't work, not for six more months and then how do we pay for sitters? He hated doing it, but we didn't have another choice."

The last words rang out in Tommy Ray's head as he sat on the bench in the hospital. Tommy Ray was no Sherlock Holmes, he knew that. But he was pretty good at finding bad guys and pretty good at reading people. These people weren't thieves, they were just poor. Nobody had been hurt, which helped the situation. They were not evil people, just lost.

A doctor escorted Maria and her baby over to a bench directly across from Tommy Ray in the waiting room. It was clear that she had been crying for some time, but had found a way to regain her composure. Her makeup was smeared and her hair was frazzled, but she managed to force a smile at Tommy Ray. For the moment, the world moved past them in a frantic pace, but neither seemed to notice.

"What happens now?" Maria asked quietly as she moved a sleeping Sarah from her left shoulder to her right.

"Where's the gun that he used?" Tommy Ray asked which forced an unexpected laugh from Maria that startled Sarah.

After Sarah put her head back down, Maria continued. "It was a stapler," she said, increasing the smile. "He didn't want to hurt anybody, but he knew he had to make it look and sound convincing. So he just gave it a good click in his jacket pocket and it sounded like the cocking of a gun."

Even in all his years on the force, Tommy Ray had never heard that one. The two of them just sat there trying not to laugh for fear of waking Sarah for a minute before Tommy Ray continued.

"There was another person involved. A guy was pushing Jason Lee's car out of the way from a train. Who is he?" This was the real reason he was here. Jason Lee was a minor problem. Now, Tommy Ray just wanted to find this other man and see if he also destroyed IT's fence.

"I don't know," Maria said. "When JL came home, he looked like he had seen a ghost. When I asked him what happened, he told me about how some guy had nearly gotten hit by a train pushing his car out of the way. He had been crying because he was so embarrassed by not being able doing anything but just try to get away. I guess he was ashamed."

At that moment, two uniform officers exited the elevator doors that were next to the waiting room that Tommy Ray and Maria were sitting in. They walked straight to Tommy Ray, ignoring Maria completely.

"I am officer John Stevens, and this is Mark Trawles," the first officer said. "We were told that you found the suspect in those thefts that have been hitting local gas stations."

Tommy Ray took a moment and looked at Maria. Her head was down as she clung to Sarah as if she might lose her.

"Nah," Tommy Ray said, "wrong guy."

Maria's head was up in an instant, staring at Tommy Ray.

Officer Trawles said, "But we were told that you had positively identified him. Didn't you call it in?"

Tommy Ray wasn't sure of a lot of things in his life. He wasn't sure what his son was doing right now. He wasn't sure who this crazy man in the pictures was. He wasn't sure where his job would lead him, if he had voted for the right President or if he was even real and this was all some imaginary hoax that someone was playing on him. Heck, he wasn't sure what he was going to do when he walked out of the doors of this hospital. But, he was sure of one thing and one thing only. And that was what he wanted to say next.

"Sorry, I got the wrong guy. This one's completely innocent."

40

The feeling was hard to describe, something that had been lost and now returned but still seemed foreign somehow. As Tommy Ray walked to his car, he couldn't quite understand it. His walk was quicker than before and his steps more determined, but that wasn't quite it. Whatever it was, something was different and Tommy Ray couldn't quite figure that out. For a detective, that was something.

He drove out of the hospital and decided to drive back to the scene with the train that he had seen so many times on video. As Tommy Ray pulled up, the traffic light and railroad looked no different than it had the previous day. He parked the car along the far right of the road and turned on his hazard lights. Then Tommy Ray got out and walked to the train tracks. He found nothing different than normal train tracks. He turned to look at the traffic light and still found nothing.

That feeling kept nagging at him, but still Tommy Ray couldn't decipher it. As he turned away from the light and looked past the railroad tracks, he could see the convenience store where the "theft" had taken place.

With a little smile forming, Tommy Ray decided to go and look one more time.

As Tommy Ray pulled into the parking lot, his cell phone rang. Many people had either songs or ear-bleeding ring tones that annoyed anyone within hearing range, but Tommy Ray preferred the default ring and had never changed it. He almost decided not to answer it before looking and seeing the number. He son, Daniel, was calling.

"Daniel, is everything okay?" he asked cursing himself for beginning the talk like a cop, not a dad.

"Dad," Daniel answered not noticing, "I made the basketball team. I'm the second string forward!" Tommy Ray realized at that moment what he had been feeling before, because now the feeling exploded inside him. He was happy, genuinely happy. This was something he had not felt in a long time.

"Tell me about the tryouts," Tommy Ray replied. He sat and listened to Daniel talk for what seemed like forever. The whole world could have passed right in front of his car and Tommy Ray would not have cared. He hung on to Daniel's every word and felt his heart beat faster than it had in a long time. After the morning he had and now this, Tommy Ray felt that the world was finally starting to make sense to him. Everything seemed in place.

After telling Daniel how proud he was, Tommy Ray got out of his car and walked into the convenience store thinking how great his day was turning out to be. It wasn't before he walked down the aisle to get a bottle of water in the back refrigerated section that he realized someone was pointing a gun at him.

41

Calvin stared out of the window in his office. The concept of having his own office was mind boggling all by itself. The fact it had a window was over the top. His view was of a Toyota dealership and a strip center complete with a Tuesday Morning, Big Lots, a store that looked a lot like a big and tall women's clothing store although the sign had fallen down several months ago, a comic book store, and a Chinese buffet. Ah, but it was a window, though.

When Calvin had entered the office, he had fully expected to have the Perfect Storm, also known as Candace, approach him about being late and grind him down in front of the employees. He had expected it so much that he had taken the stairs instead of the elevator in order to give him more time to rehearse his excuse, but as he walked past the Storm's office, Candace just smiled and waved to him as if she were the local crossing guard and Calvin was driving slower than the allotted 20mph. Uncomfortable with the new and improved Hurricane of the Century, Calvin smiled and nodded to her before bolting directly to his new office.

Calvin walked through the maze of cubicles thinking of Candace in a school crossing guard outfit trying to get upset kindergarten children across the street to school by telling them there is no crying in crossing a street, there is no crying in crossing the street when his cell phone rang snapping him back to reality.

"Calvin, its Karli. We have an issue with the copy machine. Can we move the meeting back an hour?"

"What meeting?"

"The new marketing strategy meeting. Candace sent an email about it yesterday. Did you get it?"

Calvin was not sure why they needed copies for the meeting, but decided that he should leave that part alone. He was sure, though, that he had no idea about a meeting and needed time to prepare. "Sure. We can move it back an hour or more if you need. Can you let the others know?" Calvin replied.

"Yeah, I'll let them know. By the way, did you have any of the competitor's products? I just thought it might be a nice way to compare their product and ours. If not, I can go get them."

Calvin still wasn't exactly what they were meeting about since he hadn't read the email, but presumably it had to do with their competition. Calvin the Super-sleuth strikes again. One thing that hadn't changed for Calvin yet regardless of office or position: He wanted every chance in the world he could find to get out of the office.

"No," Calvin replied. "I will go get them right now. Just get the copies ready and let the others know."

"Great. Glad you are with us!" the last comment coming from Karli sounded more forced than heartfelt, but Calvin half expected that.

Calvin took the elevator this time so that he could get out quicker. He had to find some baby formula and also wanted his usual Diet Pepsi with lime. When he reached his car, Calvin knew where he was going. There was a nice little convenience store down the road that he'd visited just the other day.

42

It wasn't clear how she was breathing, but somehow she was getting air. Janiyah had her face so far planted in the pillow that Aleesha wasn't sure how she could manage a gulp of air, much less maintain the three-hour marathon of crying that she'd witnessed. What she did know was that Janiyah was hearing the voice again.

Aleesha had been home on the phone when Janiyah had rushed through the door in full panic mode. As a consultant for a human resources company, Aleesha was able to work many days from home even though most of those days were spent on the phone. There had been a lot of traveling, but Aleesha wanted to be home more this year than ever before when Janiyah went back to school. Fortunately, she was home today.

Janiyah had immediately gone into a full face plant into her pillow so her words were hard to understand. It didn't help that they came with tears and the most mournful cry Aleesha had ever heard from her daughter. When she could hear a few words as Janiyah forced the pain from her tongue, Aleesha realized she was telling her the voice had come back.

Aleesha began crying, too, but tried to hold as much in as she could. She knew Janiyah needed her to be strong and there was anger there as well, helping hold back the tears. Aleesha had long believed that this had all been a prank, but neither she nor the investigator the school had hired had been able to find anything out. There had been a rumor from a school board member about a couple of other pranks that had been played out near the same time, but they were focused around the school newspaper and computers, not voices in the bathroom.

"What, Momma?" Janiyah whispered as she turned over to rest her head on the pillow. "I thought I heard you curse,"

"Sorry, baby," Aleesha replied, not really knowing what to say next. How does a mom ask her daughter if she's crazy?

"Mom."

"Yes?"

"I heard it again."

"I know, dear."

"He wants me to save someone."

"Who?"

"He didn't say."

The tears began flowing and all Aleesha's strength drained away in that instance. Janiyah sat up into her mothers' arms and they held each other tight.

"I thought it was a prank, Mommy," Janiyah said, the tears slurring her words. "But the voice sounded just like it did the last time, so I panicked."

"I am so sorry, dear." Aleesha held her daughter tighter.

"Who am I supposed to save and why?"

"I don't know, dear, but we will figure this out together."

The two just held each other tight, crying on each other's shoulders. Between the tears, Aleesha heard the front door open and close and knew that David was home. She began to cry just a little harder.

Janiyah's father, David, had refused to believe that someone could carry out a prank like that. David's grandfather had gone senile early in David's life. He got to witness firsthand how a crazy family member could ruin a family. His father had lost his compassion and his heart. Too many times he would see his dad just sitting on the chair, staring out the window, not caring what went on around him. Those times had usually come right after David's grandfather had an "episode."

He wasn't sure what moment in his life had been harder, but there were two memories that vied for that position. The first had been when he caught his father crying. The same man he had always looked up to had just hung up the phone after talking to his mother. His father and mother were shopping in the mall when he began to attack a security guard. Apparently, he felt the security guard was spying on him. His grandfather had been immediately sent to the psychiatric hospital. The second moment happened when David's grandfather, now free from the hospital after a year's stay, had run in front of a moving bus, challenging it to a fight. He lost the fight and the family had been free. Again, his father had cried. But this time, there was a relief in his father's pain. David knew the toll that senility could take.

That had led to David putting his daughter straight into the hospital upon hearing about the voices. Aleesha had not been able to stop him and had sat back and watched as her baby had to be led down the hallway in the hospital with her helplessly watching. It had been painful, to the point that David and Aleesha hadn't talked for nearly three months after Janiyah had left.

43

By the time he reached the convenience store, Calvin was thirsty. He had a long-standing fetish with Diet Pepsi with Lime that hit him several times a day. Today, the urge was in full gear. He knew he needed to find the baby formula for work and that he would have to make note of where the shelves were located at and on what shelf baby formula was stored so that he could report back to the team. This marketing seemed minor to many, but played a major role in a products development. Calvin decided that the Diet Pepsi should go first and then he could concentrate on the product.

Calvin parked and quickly climbed out of the car. Fortunately, there were only three customers in the store when he walked and they weren't bothering anybody. It actually seemed a little quieter than it had in the past. Calvin chose not to walk down the aisle with the two men, or the back way with the girl, but chose the only other open aisle. As he walked down, Calvin suddenly realized something and turned with a jerk. It seemed to startle everyone around.

"Sorry," Calvin said to the man staring at him across the shelves. "I just found what I needed." With a quick movement, Calvin reached down and grabbed the baby formula that was on the bottom shelf right next to nose spray and dog food. Taking note of the area of the shelf, Calvin walked to the back of the store to get his drink from the refrigerated section, and then walked back down the same aisle that he had just come from.

It seemed odd that nobody in the store had moved since he had gotten there. The clerk, a woman from India, began to check Calvin out by taking the drink from his hand. Her hand was shaking and she refused to look Calvin in the eyes.

"Is everything okay?" Calvin asked.

The clerk, whose name badge said Shaeen, just smiled at Calvin and nodded. Still, nobody had moved, much less said a word. It wasn't until Shaeen told Calvin the amount that he realized what was happening.

"Nine dollars and eleven cents," she told Calvin.

He was about to complain about the high price when it hit him: 911. He knew he should just walk out the door and call for help. Every part of his being said to turn and go. But Calvin stood there for just a moment, frozen, before he looked at the little TV monitor behind the clerk that showed the store. A man was there, facing another man who was holding what appeared to be a very old revolver. Calvin had to leave, he had to get help and he knew it. Every part of his being screamed run. But for some unknown reason that Calvin felt must have been the culmination of the week's events, Calvin turned around to face the men.

"God wants me to help," he told himself as he walked towards the two men.

44

"What the f—?" was all the man could get out before he stepped back away from Tommy Ray and held the gun towards the new man. Tommy Ray had seen a lot in his time. Never had he seen as idiotic a move as this man coming towards a gunman. To Tommy Ray's astonishment, the man kept coming.

The gunman now stood at the far end of the aisle, his gun pointed directly at the new guy as he continued to exchange glances between him and Tommy Ray. The gunman had taken Tommy Ray's gun and stuffed it in his coat pocket while he held his own gun out. There was very little space between the two men and plenty of space for the gunman to turn on Tommy Ray if he made a move. Basically, Tommy Ray was screwed. So much for having a great day.

As Tommy Ray looked at this new man, he swore he looked familiar but he just couldn't figure out how. The stress of the situation was getting in the way of his thoughts. At least the woman in the back had stopped screaming and was now just standing still. The distraction should have given the store clerk enough space and time to find and click the silent alarm. Police officers would be here soon; Tommy Ray just needed to buy some time.

"What are you doing?" the gunman asked the new guy, getting agitated at the new development.

"I'm here to help," the new guy said.

Tommy Ray couldn't believe his ears. Here to help? Help who?

"I don't need help, I just need you to get back," the gunman said.

"Who are you helping?" Tommy Ray blurted out. He almost cursed himself for saying anything, but he just needed to know.

"Everyone," the man said. "God said to save His people, so I am saving His people."

Had Tommy Ray expected that answer, it would have been the ideal time to jump the gunman. He, along with the others in the store, froze for a second, trying to determine if they had really just heard what they'd just heard. By the time Tommy Ray had snapped out of it, so had the gunman.

"Who said save who? How are you, going to save these people?" the gunman asked.

For the first time since this drama began playing out, Tommy Ray had begun to sweat. He noticed, too, that the gunman's demeanor was a little less confident with this new man standing so close. The hand holding the gun had begun to shake slightly.

"Really," the man began, "God told me to save His people. I guess that means you, too."

And with that Tommy Ray had finally had it. A gun on him was one thing but hostages and screaming women were other things. Now a man was trying to save everyone, including a gunman. No, not happening.

"Are you crazy?" Tommy Ray yelled to the man. "What are you thinking?" Tommy Ray had forgotten about the gun and now was focused on this new guy. "You had the chance to get out. You could have even gone for help or called nine-one-one. Maybe, even with half a brain, you could have even driven away and just not looked back." Tommy Ray was into it now moving his hands around as he pointed to the new guy and his car and the gunman as he spoke. "But, NO. You, in all your infinite wisdom and I'm sure your experience with crazy men, decided to stay put and walk directly up to dumbass here and use the God card?"

"Who you calling crazy," the gunman asked, but Tommy Ray and the new man ignored the cry.

Now the new guy looked upset as he turned and walked toward Tommy Ray as if a gun was not pointed at him at all. "Listen, if you had the week I had, you would do the same. First, God yells at me to save his people while I am in the restroom. So I ignore him. Then, he sends a twenty-foot dinosaur down from the sky to wreck my car. As if that wasn't enough, I'm nearly electrocuted trying to get these two guys off my car."

The new guy was really into it now, his breathing was increasing and his face was getting red as he continued.

"So, if that was not bad enough, then I was nearly hit by a train, just trying to help a guy move his car. And you know what I got? Not a single thanks. No, not one. But what I did get was from this priest telling me to believe in second chances and follow. So you know what I'm going to do, mister? I'm going to follow and do what I'm supposed to do. See, ever since I started believing, everything else has worked out." The finger-pointing and red-faced new man finally took a deep breath and exhaled.

"I'm Tommy Ray," the detective said as he held out his hand toward the new guy. "I've been looking for you."

Taken back a little, Calvin said, "Calvin James," and the two men shook hands.

In the distance, police sirens increased in volume as they got closer to the store.

45

The clock lied. It showed that an hour had passed, but it had only felt like a few minutes. As Shaeen sat down on the floor of the Quickstop, her heart had finally slowed down. The officer who was questioning her had tried to get her out of the store, but Shaeen had refused. Her head was swimming with what she had just witnessed and her legs were much too weak to walk. Instead, the officer sat down next to her and leaned back on the register counter.

"Okay, just so I am sure of what you said," Officer Bennett said, "he said he didn't mean to shoot anybody, it was clearly an accident?"

With a heavy sigh, Shaeen looked to the aisle where the cop and the crazy man and the gunman had been standing.

"It all changed when you guys showed up."

"How did it change, Shaeen?"

"Well, it started with the crazy guy who was hearing God."

"God."

"Yeah, God. He tried to stop the gunman from doing anything bad, and ended up screwing the whole thing up."

"Well, it sounds like he might have saved the guy as well."

"Go figure."

"How about you tell me the story from when we showed up?"

"Okay." Shaeen paused trying to think how it started. "It began with 'Oh, God.'"

"Oh, God!" the gunman yelled as a big, black truck with the words SWAT rolled into the parking lot.

Calvin, Tommy Ray, and the gunman looked out into the parking lot to see the truck park at the far end of the lot, facing the store. They could tell when the back door opened and several officers got out, but they were not sure how many.

Tommy Ray had that sinking feeling that things were about to get crazy.

There were already several police cruisers and three unmarked police cars. The police cruisers had been parked between the store and the gas pumps as they stood nearly bumper-to-bumper across the store's front. Nobody had come between the store and the cars.

"Oh God, oh God, oh God," the gunman kept saying as he sank down in the aisle where he and the other men had been standing.

Calvin and Tommy Ray looked out the window to watch the circus.

Shaeen stood in the same spot throughout all of it. She turned to look at the parking lot, then turned back to see the men. She had completely forgotten about the woman in the back corner by the soda machine until the woman began to cry again.

"Stop crying, just stop crying," the gunman screamed at the woman as he held his hands to his head, the gun still in his right hand. "I can't think."

"What's your name?" the voice came like a shock. Everyone turned to look at Tommy Ray, he asked again.

"John," was all the gunman would give.

"Just let her go, John. She is too stressed to be here right now and it will look good for you in dealing with the officers outside. Just let her go."

John looked up at Calvin for a second almost pleading with his eyes for help.

Calvin took the chance. "You should let her go. You have us and we're staying. Let her go."

John didn't answer so much as motion with his gun for the lady to leave. It took the woman a few tentative steps before she realized he was serious. Then she took off at a full run, nearly crashing into the sliding doors before they opened. It was at that moment that John, and the others, realized that they had never even locked the doors. Tommy Ray tried not to smile at the thought, but it was hard not to.

Calvin sat down in the aisle across from John, but Tommy Ray chose to stay standing. As he looked out to the parking lot, he watched as the woman was ushered behind the SWAT truck. He wasn't sure who was in charge right now, but he figured she was telling them what was going on. After a few moments, the SWAT team moved into positions behind the cars and to the sides of the building. It looked to Tommy Ray like they didn't like what she'd said.

"John, if you want to get out of this alive, we have to think fast," Tommy Ray said.

"I just needed some money," John exclaimed. "I just needed some cash. Nobody was going to get hurt, just some cash and I was out of here."

There was a long pause as Tommy Ray thought about what to say next.

John beat him to it. "How is God going to save me now?" He looked at Calvin.

To Calvin's credit thought Tommy Ray, he didn't budge. He kept his eyes on John the whole time as he spoke to him.

"I don't know, but he will," Calvin began. "A few days ago, I was a mess and somehow through the most chaotic time of my life, I found my family again, got promoted, and feel like a man again just because He gave me a second chance."

"From a voice in a restroom?" John asked. "Sounds like a trick."

"Maybe, but it's worked so far."

"Oh, my God!" Shaeen screamed.

Tommy Ray took his eyes off of the two men and looked back outside. There were SWAT team members moving and a few heavily armed ones coming directly toward the door. John stood up to look at what Shaeen had screamed at when a red light froze on his forehead, causing him to back up until he was flat against the shelves next to Calvin. Several other lights danced around the store as well, searching for a resting spot.

Tommy Ray began to yell for everyone to stop, but it was Calvin who stood up to act. Unfortunately, he still held on to the baby formula. With all the excitement, he gripped it too hard, and it burst on the floor. Cursing to himself, Calvin still tried to get up, but slipped on the baby formula. As he fell, he reached for the shelves to brace himself. One broke, sending candy bars in every direction and throwing himself and John to the ground.

As John landed, he reached out to brace himself but dropped the gun when he fell. John landed with a thud and the gun landed with a bang. Tommy Ray ducked out of habit and Shaeen screamed. More importantly, the SWAT team that had begun to move stopped in their tracks. There was a moment of stillness as everyone waited to see what would happen next. Again, it was Shaeen's scream that got people moving again.

"Oh my God!" she screamed, pointing at Calvin.

Tommy Ray looked down to see Calvin lying on his back, eyes closed and blood pouring out of his shirt. He reacted quickly. "John, lay down on the floor with your hands on your head," he yelled as he reached out and picked up the gun, stuffing it into his pocket.

"But it was an accident!" John exclaimed, staring at Calvin.

"I know, but you have to do this or he's going to bleed to death," Tommy Ray replied as he ran to the door.

John did as he was told and rolled over, and Tommy Ray ran to the door.

"It's over, he's down. A man's been shot."

"The next thing I know," Shaeen said, "you guys came rushing in here and took those two men away." She kept looking down the aisle where the men had been. Drops of blood were still present along the floor and part of the shelves. "Where did they all go?"

"The officer went with the victim, and the suspect is in custody," the officer said as he stood up to leave. "By the way, he saved him," the officer said.

"What?" Shaeen asked as she looked up at the officer.

"Yeah. The SWAT team was told by the lady in here that the gunman was crazy and was going to shoot someone."

"He wasn't crazy, well, maybe, but he didn't act it. He just looked scared."

"Well, they'd decided to move in and take him out anyway. This Calvin guy probably saved the gunman's life."

Shaeen watched as the officer walked out and a paramedic walked up to her. The day had been such a blur; she was almost numb to any emotions. But as the paramedic reached her, Shaeen began to think of Calvin and how he had walked into the aisle as if he really could help. Somehow, it had all ended in such a disaster. If he had really just saved the gunman, who was going to save him?

46

Tommy Ray recognized the hospital as soon as he stepped out of the ambulance. He had come along with the EMT to take Calvin to the hospital out of some sense of responsibility. He wasn't really sure why, but knew he wanted to see this through.

The drive had only taken a few minutes but had felt like hours. Tommy Ray had a tough job, but he knew he could never do what the EMT did. The medic in the back kept constant vigil with Calvin, relaying the information to his partner and to Tommy Ray about his status. Most of it was beyond Tommy Ray, he just nodded to the medic as if he knew what he was saying.

As they pulled Calvin out of the ambulance and began to rush him to the emergency room, Tommy Ray could see that the spot of blood on Calvin's shirt had grown during the ambulance ride, and had not stopped yet. As if in a trance, Tommy Ray followed the growing posse of doctors and nurses as the EMT handed off Calvin to them. They spoke in a foreign tongue to each other about readings and pressures and something about the placement of the bullet, but Tommy Ray was too tired to focus on them. He just followed the pack as it raced through the labyrinth of hallways.

When they reached a set of double doors marked personnel only, one of the nurses stopped and stood in front of Tommy Ray preventing him from going any farther. "Do you know the victim?"

Tommy Ray reached into his pocket and pulled out his badge, dropping a piece of folded paper. "I am an officer who was there when it happened," he said as he reached down to grab the paper. When he stood back up and looked through the tiny windows in the door, giving him a view where they had taken Calvin, he saw nothing but an empty hallway.

"You need to wait in the lounge. We will keep you updated," the nurse answered and promptly turned and vanished through the double doors.

Tommy Ray stood in the hallway, staring through the windows, hoping to see something. He was almost thankful when only an empty hallway stared back. After giving up the chance of seeing anything else, Tommy Ray walked to the lounge and dropped into one of the chairs. He still held the paper that had fallen out of his pocket. He realized what it was before he opened it: He had taken the picture of the man at the train tracks with him and must have folded it and put it in his pocket at some point during the chaos.

As he looked at the picture, the face was still not completely identifiable. Even still, the outline of the body and the features were obvious. The man staring back at him was the man who was dying in the emergency room down an empty hallway.

47

"I'm not crazy, I'm not," Janiyah yelled at her father. All hope in creating a peaceful negotiation had been lost when David had been contacted by the school attendance office stating that Janiyah had "missed" her last three classes of the day. After everything they had been through, it was a quick decision to pack up his things and leave the office for the day. What happened when he got home was more of a whirlwind than a family discussion.

First, the obvious hint that something was up had shown when Aleesha and Janiyah came downstairs putting on the most obvious fake smiles they could muster. The fact that both of their faces were puffy from crying and each had running mascara that had been quickly wiped away but stilled showed in outline form on their cheeks.

Second came the "Everything's fine" routine, followed by "It was just a bad day at school, but everything is fine now" reply. Both ladies moved past him as his beloved tried with all her might to not make eye contact. That alone was a bad sign. They moved to the kitchen, stopping by the living room long enough to turn the television on and tune in to the news channel.

It was the oldest trick in the book, or at least in their household. Nothing was better than twenty-four hours of news and David's craving just magnified every time it was on. But this time, he fought the desire and moved into the kitchen with them.

The third step was the most obvious. Janiyah began to break down and cry into her mother's waiting arms. Not that he ever pretended to be a great detective, but that performance pretty much ended any kind of game they were trying to play. The next part began the whirlwind and it only took one simple little question that David would regret coming out of his mouth.

"What happened?"

A half hour later and David still had no idea exactly what had happened. He put together that Janiyah was hearing voices again, but the crying and screaming had prevented him from understanding exactly what she was saying. Somehow, Aleesha understood everything. He thought it must be one of those women things that they understood in each other when they were crying, kind of like going to the bathroom in groups, or "I'll be ready in a few minutes" takes two hours and "we need to talk" which really meant he was only supposed to shut up and listen.

It was hard to see your baby like this. It was even harder to see it for a second time. There was a feeling of being powerless to stop the pain, clueless on what to say next or what to do, and downright mad at God for putting your baby through this. Powerless and clueless are not comfortable thoughts for a father. So, not knowing how to handle it, he decided to try to solve it. That was when the explosion came, when David brought up about going back to see the doctors.

"Really, Dad, I'm not crazy. I know I heard the voice again, but it seemed so real."

"That was the same thing you said last time," he replied.

Aleesha had tried to help, holding her daughter in her arms, but had lost her words in her own tears. Finally, she had let go and moved into the living room to try to regroup. This had left Janiyah and her father to deal with the situation.

"I'm just saying," he continued, "we should think about help before this becomes a major issue. It's not like before."

"Those other voices were different," Janiyah argued. "This was the voice that I heard last time. I know you think I've been hearing all these different voices my whole life, but this one was the exact same as last time."

"And what did it say?"

There was the pause that put the tension to a new level. The pause told him everything. Still, he waited to hear her say it.

"Save my people."

"Not again."

"Yes, again."

David wanted to hold his baby, he wanted to cry, he wanted to tell her it was all right, and he still wanted to call the doctors. However, the pain and the confusion had left him numb. Instead, he just stood there and looked at her, clueless as what to say next. That was when Aleesha screamed.

"Oh my God, oh my God," she was screaming over and over as she came into the kitchen. "Come here now," she said to both of them as she pulled Janiyah's arm, followed by her body, into the living room. The television was on and still tuned to the all news channel, but a familiar looking place was on the screen.

"That's the hospital down the road," Aleesha said.

Nobody replied, they just watched the screen, listening. It was almost a reprieve to think of something else other than the fact that your daughter was crazy. The reporter was a tall, brunette female who looked Hispanic but spoke in perfect English. She was standing in front of the hospital as she spoke.

"The victim of the shooting has fallen into a coma due to blood loss. His family is with him now. Again, his name is Calvin James and he is married with two children."

"Sylvia," an off-screen voice was heard that must have come from the anchors, "do they expect him to pull through?"

"The prognoses does not look good right now, but—"

"Why are we watching this?" Janiyah exclaimed.

"Shh, baby, they'll get back to it, I'm sure."

The voice behind the scenes came back. "Tell us exactly again what the victim said prior to the shooting."

"He said he was told by God that he had to save his people."

"Save his people?"

"Yes, but get this: According to my sources, the SWAT team was prepared to go in and take out the gunman. So it appears that Mr. James actually saved him by taking the bullet himself."

Aleesha turned the television off as she stood looking at David and her baby.

"What now?"

"Mom, I have to go down there. I don't know why, but I think I have to be there for him."

"David, what do you think?"

David just stood there for a minute stunned at what he had just seen and heard. Somewhere in the back of his mind, he really wanted to believe. He wanted to believe that God was speaking to her. He wanted to believe that there was a purpose for all the pain. But, most of all, he wanted to believe that his daughter was not crazy.

"I'll get the keys," he said.

48

"That's him, I swear that's the guy," Ben said, pointing to one of the many television screens displayed on the wall in front of him. Jerry was trying to keep Ben quiet so as not to create a scene in front of the customers, but Ben was adamant.

"I'm telling you, I saw his face, and I remember it. That's the guy we punked in the airport."
"Calm down, Ben. I've never seen you like this."

"You're stupid 'save my people' crap. Look what happened to this guy."

"Whoa, you think that was because of us?"

"Yes. They aren't sure if he is going to make it."

"You really think that is because of us?"

Ben turned to look directly into Jerry's eyes. "If we did not cause this, then who did?"

Tommy Ray had passed exhaustion hours ago. He'd had a nice quiet morning with a sure-fire lead and had ended up with two trips to the hospital and had nearly been shot. Now, he sat in a waiting room as chaos ensued around him.

Calvin's family had arrived and gone directly into his room. The children had come out quickly, but the wife had stayed in the room. Both kids looked really upset. As if that was not bad enough, the media had now grown, causing a circus atmosphere outside. Local officers had been called in to help control the growing situation while trying to give the kids a little peace. One photographer had snuck past the line of defense and had made it to the waiting room and snapped three quick pictures of the kids holding each other before he was roughly escorted back outside.

To make matters worse, an African-American couple and their daughter had come into the room being escorted by a doctor and were now visibly arguing with each other, although they were trying desperately to keep it to themselves and yet by trying not to create a distraction, they were creating a distraction. Worse off, the doctor's name badge was the same name on the list of doctors in the hallway, only his was listed under the psyche ward.

Tommy Ray still had not spoken with Calvin's wife yet, and was waiting for her to return to the kids before approaching her. Still, what do you say to a wife whose husband just got shot trying to save some dumbass robber's life because he thinks God told him to. Yeah, today started out so nice and quiet.

"I don't know what I'm supposed to do," Janiyah tried to scream but forced her voice low so nobody but her mom and dad would hear her.

"Well, we're here. We have to do something," he father said as he turned his attention to the door to the room where the man in the comma was being attended. "He can't hear or see you, so this may not be the best time."

"I know it is, Daddy, this is the time. I'm just not sure how."

"We will figure it out together, sweetie," her mother said. "Somehow, we will figure this out."

Just then the door to the man's room opened and a woman came out. Janiyah watched as she went directly to the two children sitting in the corner of the waiting room. A man, who had been sitting on the other side of the room, had gone directly over to them and begun talking. The family seemed to just sit and listen to the man without talking, almost as if they were petrified in their tracks.

"We need to go talk with them right now," Janiyah said.

Her father had already moved before the Janiyah or her mother could react.

"Pardon me," he began by interrupting their conversation. "My daughter needs just a moment of your time."

"Right now?" the man standing asked, as if trying to protect the ones sitting down.

Janiyah had come up quickly behind her father. She began to speak, but the tears had begun again which quenched her voice from speaking. Now, all of them were looking at her, waiting for her to speak again. Janiyah cleared her throat and began again. "I heard the voice, too."

It wasn't a green field of flowers, or a pearly gate. No, it wasn't really anything. More like fog without the fog. He felt as if he were standing in a closet made of glass in which nobody could hear him. Not that there was anybody out there, just that he had no voice. He screamed, yelled, banged, and kicked at nothing, but no sound came out.

Finally, he could see a dark image come across the horizon. As it came closer, it actually seemed to grow smaller. It made a sound, some kind of sound, but it was so muffled that Calvin couldn't make it out. He cried out desperately for it to make some kind of sense, to speak clear, but it refused to acknowledge him.

He tried to run, but couldn't move. He screamed again with no voice. He jumped and waved, but his feet never left the ground and his arms fell hopelessly at his side. The figure moved closer and then farther away. Calvin swore it almost looked like a little girl, but that made no sense. He just kept screaming and yelling until he realized it was hopeless.

Hadn't he done what he was supposed to? Hadn't he done what was asked? Now, he lay here powerless. But as he began to stop yelling and pounding and jumping, Calvin realized something else, there was something missing. Something he couldn't quite put a finger on, but he knew it was missing.

Calvin stood there and watched as the figure moved closer and farther away. Occasionally, there was movement that almost looked like an arm or hand flying around, but it was so blurry that he wasn't really sure what he was looking at. Calvin took a deep breath that really didn't feel like a breath at all and closed his eyes. Darkness, stillness, calm.

That was it. He was calm. No pain, no tension, no feelings of what if or what had I done. Instead, Calvin felt great. The years of living under a dark cloud were missing and instead a feeling of something else. Pleasure, no. Happiness, no. What it seemed like and felt like was good old-fashioned calm. It was hard to understand, but Calvin felt like the weight of the world had been lifted from his shoulders.

It was precisely at that moment that the big bright light came right at him and the thumping began.

49

Jerry was on the phone trying to get hold of someone at the news station. Ben sat on the couch, staring in disbelief. Somehow they had pulled off two of the greatest pranks ever and now those two pranks had merged together. The coverage was outstanding and crystal clear. They could see people walking in and out of the hospital right behind the Channel 5 reporter. That was also how they saw "her."

"Got someone," Jerry said as he turned to away from Ben and the television in order to hear the person on the other line better.

Ben wondered what he was saying, but decided he didn't want any part of the conversation. Things were getting crazy. First they find out the man they pranked in the airport is lying in a comma in the hospital, then they see the girl that they pranked twice in school walking behind the reporter and into the hospital.

At first, he and Jerry thought that she was going to the psych ward, but they remembered that it was located on a different area all together. It was a few minutes later that the reporter had come across with some inside information to help them. She reported that someone inside the hospital witnessed an African-American girl going into the victim's room. Ben and Jerry would have screamed or fallen over laughing, or yelled to the world "Look what we did," but they couldn't. They were immobilized on the couch, staring in disbelief at what was happening right before their eyes.

Right after that, Jerry decided to call the press and let them know about the girl "anonymously."

"It's done," Jerry said as he jumped the back of the couch and sat down next to Ben. Precisely at that moment, the reporter was holding her earpiece closer to her so she could hear.

"Things are about to get crazy," Jerry said.

As if they weren't crazy enough already, Ben thought.

50

There were no answers. Nothing telling her this is it, here is what you do. No instruction manual, no voices, nothing. Janiyah stood inside the room, just a step past the doorway, looking at some overweight white man with a bunch of tubes stuck in his nose and running down to places she did not want to think about. The nurse that brought her in had gone over to check the monitors and had adjusted the man's air tube and then walked out, leaving the two of them alone.

Already it seemed as if the man were having more difficulty breathing. The pump, or whatever it was, had been barely working as it moved up and down slowly, but now moved up and down in shorter, more erratic movements since the nurse had left. Janiyah thought she should go get her, but somehow felt compelled to stay with the man and see this through.

As Janiyah walked up to the seemingly lifeless body before her, she lost complete track of the speech she had memorized on the way over to the hospital. She hoped that by telling him her story and about their mutual voice, he would suddenly heal up and be all better and the craziness in her life would make sense. But, somehow, Janiyah knew that it would never be that simple. She stood over him as if he could see her and tried to talk to him as if he could hear her speak.

"Hello. My name is Janiyah. I know you can't hear me right now, but I have to tell you this story. It may seem crazy for me to be speaking to a man I never met who is lying in a coma, but I've been called crazy for a few years now and I am kind of getting used to it. I heard the voice too, twice now. At first I thought it was a joke, but the voice kept playing in my mind and in my dreams. It's kind of weird, actually. When I was a kid, I kept hearing voices. I told my mom and dad, but they just thought it was one of those imaginary friends. But the voices seemed so real, like they were actually talking to me.

"By the way, the voices aren't scary, really. They almost seem like angels looking out for you. One time, they said to stay inside the house. Later, we found out that a child molester had been found wandering our neighborhood. Nobody had been hurt since none of the kids had gone outside. Another time when I was scared of a storm, they spoke to me and told me it was about to pass. Ten minutes later, it was gone. I swear the voices are real and from someone watching over me, but my parents and all those doctors keep telling me that they are from my imagination. It didn't really matter until today.

"As I got older, my parents got a little wigged out and told me to stop playing pretend. They even took me to a shrink. So, little by little the voices started going away. Until one day, I realized they weren't there anymore, or at least I couldn't hear them. You might think it sounds good, but it wasn't. It was kind of lonely, like friends of mine had deserted me.

"Then, one day in the bathroom at school, which really sounds much grosser than it really was, one of the voices came back. Maybe it was a joke, probably it was, but I didn't realize how much I missed the voices. When it spoke it was a shock and I was so freaked out, but it just spoke clear to me. 'Save my people,' was all it said. And that is why I had to talk to you. It spoke to me again just recently as it had spoken to you. Maybe we have something in common."

Janiyah looked down at the man who seemed to be getting whiter as she stood over him. The air pump that led to his breathing was now straining and the monitor connected to it was starting to beep. The signal thingy that had been moving up and down was starting to go flatter and flatter. Janiyah had no idea what was going on, but this seemed bad.

"You have to wake up!" she screamed. "Help!" she yelled but there was a commotion outside the door. Janiyah turned to look at the man as if she could do anything but suddenly felt completely powerless. All her hopes had resided in this moment, this tiny little chance that she could help this man, and now it looked like she was going to fail and let him die. She began to yell at the man and yell for help, but the commotion outside had grown louder.

Suddenly, the door to the room burst open and a bright light filled the room.

51

Tommy Ray noticed him first and reacted before anyone else realized what was happening. The entire waiting room, including the nurses, was glued to the television and the reporter showing the chaos in front of the hospital. An unidentified source had called in and told the news crew about the girl in the room with Calvin and the voices she had heard. As the reporter spoke, more crews were showing up as their lights became evident in the background. The circus had truly come to town.

Tommy Ray took his eyes off the television so that he would not see the fiasco that was running downstairs, when he saw the movement in the corner. Someone had come up from behind the nurse's station and had moved close to Calvin's door. The man had on jeans and a Green Bay Packers T-shirt with a red baseball cap on backwards. He was trying to hide something behind him. He seemed to notice Tommy Ray as soon as Tommy Ray noticed him.

Immediately, Tommy Ray was up and racing to the man as fast as he could move. Tommy Ray had yelled for help, but knew he was the only one that could act quickly enough. When the man brought out a news camera and pointed it at Tommy Ray, he turned on the light, blinding Tommy Ray for an instant.

Tommy Ray heard commotion before he could gain his sight back. When he looked up, the father of the little girl inside the room had grabbed hold of the camera man around the waist and the two were twisting and turning as if it were a dance, all while the camera was rolling. Inside the waiting room, the kids witnessed the dance on the television, as it also played out live in front of them. Neither was sure if they should laugh or cry.

Tommy Ray jumped to help and grabbed the cameraman, trying to pull down his arms as the cameraman lifted the camera higher and higher, trying to keep it out of Tommy Ray's grasp. As the cameraman twisted, the father that was helping Tommy Ray tripped and slammed to the ground. Tommy Ray and the cameraman continued their dance until Tommy Ray tripped over the father on the ground. Tommy Ray hit the ground hard but managed to hold onto the cameraman's shirt bringing him down to, right on top of the pile. The cameraman fell towards the door and tried using it to brace himself with it. Instead, the door burst open and the camera flooded the room with light.

The cameraman was up quickly, trying to steady the camera. Both the father and Tommy Ray stood up immediately after him and lunged for the cameraman. For some reason, the cameraman had stopped, probably to keep filming, Tommy Ray thought, but it didn't matter. The moment helped as he grabbed the camera and the father tackled the man. It took a moment for Tommy Ray to find the off switch. Immediately, the room was less bright and much clearer. He wanted to turn and jump on that stupid cameraman, but the local security team had shown up finally and had hold of him. They were trying desperately to wrestle the father off him. The father had a pretty good grip on the man's neck and it was taking three of them to pry him off.

It was the girl yelling that made Tommy Ray forget about the cameraman.

"Help me, somebody help me," she was screaming as she tried to push and shove the bed causing the body to move and shake.

Tommy Ray ran to the girl ready to grab her and pull her down much like he just watched her father do to the cameraman when she pointed to it.

"You see, it's stuck, he can't get any air."

Tommy Ray looked down to see a tube that led from Calvin's face to the breathing apparatus. The tube had gotten caught under Calvin's bed and become pinched. It was still stuck as the girl tried to move the bed.

Tommy Ray went to grab the face mask off Calvin, but it wouldn't budge.

"I tried that already, it's too tight. Help me with this," the girl said as she tried lifting the bed. It took Tommy Ray more time than he wished to admit before realizing what this all meant. The suddenness of it all hit him. The man was dying.

Tommy Ray reached down and grabbed the side of the bed as he looked over at the girl who did the same.

"Ready, go" he said and the two of them lifted and pushed the bed sideways. The tube was free now and Calvin seemed no worse for the move, but his breathing was still weak and his vital signs worse. A doctor and two nurses rushed in as did Calvin's family. All stood staring wordlessly as the doctors scrambled to find out what was wrong with the man.

One nurse had rushed out and returned with scissors and cut the mask off Calvin, while another checked and rechecked his vital signs. The doctor was shouting orders and moving and prodding Calvin, but his signs grew weak. Finally, after what seemed like an eternity, the beeping ceased and the sign went flat with one continuous sound. Calvin's wife grabbed her children and held them close as the mother and father of the girl in the room held each other for dear life. Even the cameraman and the security guards were holding hands.

The doctors quickly began CPR, using a defibrillator. After countless tries, the doctor and nurses stopped and just looked down at Calvin's body. It was evident by the stillness of the air what had just happened. Everyone in the room and just outside it stood still as if the earth had ceased to rotate and stood motionless in the galaxy.

Even the air seemed to become stagnant and stale. Tommy Ray just stood there, staring, when he felt a little pressure on his right hand. He looked down to see that the girl had put her hand in his and was looking at him.

She looked up into Tommy Ray's eyes with tears rolling down her face. He was about to reach out and touch one when she moved. The girl took a step toward Calvin, pulling Tommy Ray with her. He had no willpower of his own any more. His body, mind, and soul were numb as he just let the girl lead him to the bed. Nobody behind them moved but the doctor and nurses stepped aside to allow them the side of the bed.

For a moment, Tommy Ray thought she was going to cry and then turn to him and let him hold her. He would have if she let him because secretly he wanted to hold someone as well. He thought of his son and ached painfully for him to be home, waiting for him to walk in the door and give him a huge hug. But the girl didn't turn to him; she just looked down at the body as tears strolled down her face.

It was precisely at that moment when she screamed and began banging on the body with her whole might. It had come so fast and unexpectedly that Tommy Ray didn't realize what was happening until she had gotten in four of five hits right on Calvin's chest. He pulled the girl back, holding on to her as if he was saving her life, and the two fell to the ground hard.

"He was supposed to live, we are connected, he was supposed to live!" she screamed as she turned into Tommy Ray's chest and began crying. The crying and screaming were so loud that Tommy Ray didn't hear it.

Calvin's family was so upset that they had turned away so as not to see what was happening. David and Aleesha were so upset that they held each other tight and cried themselves. The nurses and doctor were so focused on Tommy Ray and Janiyah that they forgot everything around them as well.

Tommy Ray thought he heard it, but knew it was a mistake. But when he heard it again, he knew what it was.

"Stop," he yelled. "Listen."

Then it came, stronger, faster, and louder. A beeping sound echoed in the room as the vital sign registered the progress that came from the once lifeless body. Tommy Ray and Janiyah jumped up immediately to the side of the bed. They were followed by Calvin's wife and his two children as they gathered next to them. David and Aleesha stood back still crying but with smiles spreading across their faces. The doctors and nurses just stood there in awe.

Tommy Ray wanted to say something profound, something incredible, but silently hoped the girl next to him would say it. After all, this was her moment as much as anybody's. But, the man lying before them beat them to it. As they stared down at the once lifeless body, the man who had nearly been dead a few moments before opened his eyes and looked up at all of the people surrounding him. He looked deep into their eyes and shattered the silence with his heartfelt message.

"I have to pee."

52

Janiyah sat in the waiting room for hours. Her parents had gone down to the cafeteria in the lobby, but Janiyah wasn't hungry. Calvin's family stayed in the room with him. Janiyah was hoping that maybe she could get a moment, but wasn't sure if the man had the strength.

The police officer, Tommy Ray, had spoken to Janiyah for quite a while. He did not seem to be "interviewing" her as much as just plain speaking to her. Janiyah had never really met a police officer, so her only real thoughts had been what she watched on television, but this guy seemed more genuine than that. She decided that maybe the television officers were not the norm, that maybe police officers were more like her and her parents than she gave them credit for.

During their conversation, a man and a woman came into the lobby and sat down. This lobby had been marked just for Calvin after the recent incident, so Janiyah knew that the two had received permission to be here. The man looked nice enough, but the woman looked like she could rip your heart out just by looking at you.

After nearly an hour, the family came out of Calvin's room. Calvin's wife, Becca, offered the room to the police officer and she also ushered in the two new people. She called the woman Candace, but missed the man's name as Janiyah tried not to hold the woman's look as she walked by. Then Becca came over to Janiyah.

"He wants to talk to you next," she said with a smile to Janiyah who wasn't sure if she was really ready for this but felt comforted by the woman speaking to her.

"Okay."

53

The police officer had come in first and reached to shake hands with him before he realized that Calvin was hard pressed to move his hand. They both laughed at the thought, but Calvin cut his laugh off early as the pain shot into his shoulder. The storm known as Candace walked in next with some man in tow with her. Calvin had been told that he was one of the top shareholders in the company, but Calvin did not immediately recognize him.

Calvin looked at the police officer and asked "How is that guy from the store?"

"Fine, for now. I think the judge will be lenient knowing how it happened.."

"But he's not hurt?"

"No."

"Good," Calvin said as he turned to look at Candace.

"Hi, Calvin, um . . . ." Candace began to stutter. "We are so grateful that you are okay. I told the office that everyone should wait until tomorrow to see you, but I was told this could not wait."

Candace looked to the man standing next to her, who ushered her outside with a nod of his head. He then smiled a greeting to the officer as he moved closer to Calvin's bedside. "Calvin, I heard about the incident and felt it was time that we talked," the man began as Calvin and Tommy Ray stared silently at him.

"I have had a really fortunate life. Unfortunately for me, it happened due to a near death experience when I was a child playing with one of my friends. Right after that, my father moved our family and that move turned out to be the best thing to ever happen to us. He joined a little fledgling computer company called Microsoft that just happened to take off. Anyway, I've had plenty of opportunities in my life to invest. So, when I looked you up and found where you worked, I knew I had to invest in the company so that I could help you out after what you did for me."

"What did I do for you?" Calvin asked as he tried hard to think. He had never met an investor, nor really ever cared about them. He dealt mainly with the lower part of the totem pole, not the bigwigs.

"Why would you look up Calvin to invest in a company?" Tommy Ray asked, too, the office part of him taking the lead.

"Many years ago, when I was a boy, Calvin tried to save my life."

"When?" Tommy Ray asked.

"When my foot was stuck in the train tracks."

As if the clouds broke and the sun parted ways in one instance, everything began to make sense to Calvin. "Martin?"

"Yes," the man replied, smiling.

"But, I thought you moved away from me because I nearly got you killed."

"No, it was because of the man."

"What man? It was just the two of us."

"He said he came because you were calling for help. He pulled me out and said not to be too mad at you because you tried and were scared. He said he needed you for later."

"Who was he?"

"I don't know. When I looked over to see you and found you okay on the other side of the tracks, I turned back to speak to him but he was gone. I told my parents but they said I made it up to protect you. They even went to look for footprints in the dirt, but nothing was there but my shoes."

"Then why did you move?"

"Because my dad thought I was hearing voices and he was mad about the tracks. Then he got this offer from Seattle and whoosh, we were gone."

There was silence in the room for a moment while they all digested what had happened. To Calvin, this was as important a moment in his life as the last week.

He was not the problem. He had helped his friend, not failed him. Martin was not mad, but grateful. He could have used this information a little earlier, he thought, but maybe that was how it was supposed to work.

"So, what now?" Calvin asked.

"Let me take care of your hospital stay or at least the part insurance will not take care of."

"No, I'm fine."

"Really, I want to."

"No." Calvin said. "We are fine and the insurance will take care of it. I trust in what I am doing and that I will be fine, do something else with that money."

"Are you sure?"

"Yeah."

Just then Tommy Ray stepped in next to Calvin's bed so that he could look at both Calvin and Martin.

"If you want to help someone out, I know a couple just down a couple floors that has had a hard time lately and could use some help. He just had a heart attack and they have a baby girl."

Calvin and Martin looked at each other, not as grown men in an ever-changing world, but as two kids who know they have a secret.

54

Janiyah entered the room slowly. Calvin was lying in his bed with the back of the mattress slightly upright so that it appeared he was sitting as well as lying down. He wore a smile that Janiyah could feel as well as see. As she moved to the side of his bed, she realized she had never formally met this man, yet felt like she already knew him. Still, she wasn't sure how to begin. Thankfully, he did.

"Hello, I'm Calvin James and you must be Janiyah."

"Yes. I'm glad you're alive."

"Me, too!"

There was a pause as each other tried to figure out how they should bring up what had happened. Again, it was Calvin who began.

"So, I understand that you heard Him, too."

"You think it was Him, really, or just a stupid joke that got us here?"

"Janiyah, if you knew the week I had, you would think it was Him, too."

"I'm glad. For a while I just thought I was crazy."

"Me, too."

"Really?"

"Really."

"So what do we do now?"

"I'm not sure. But, as I was lying in that coma, somehow I could see you and make out your voice. I'm not sure what it means, but I think we were brought together for a reason."

"Yeah, me, too. Maybe, somehow we are destined to help each other or something like that?"

"Or maybe, we were brought together to help those around us. And, maybe, they just don't know it yet."

Janiyah could not stop the smile from spreading even if she wanted to. Somewhere, deep inside, Janiyah felt like this was the right path and it felt good.

"So, when do we begin?"

55

Shortly after the hospital incident, Tommy Ray took two weeks off for vacation time. He spent the majority of his time visiting his son and just hanging out with him. His ex thought that it was weird, but Tommy Ray didn't care and his son was excited to see him. Upon returning home, Tommy Ray took every one of his fitness magazines and burned them. Then, for the first time in more than ten years, he went to church and on that Sunday he realized how bad a singer he truly was yet didn't care. He now attends regularly.

Jason Lee and Maria received no bill for their hospital care. When they returned home, they found that their things had been moved to a two-bedroom apartment and the rent had been paid for the next five years. There was also an envelope on the kitchen table with their names on it. The envelope seemed rather thick for a letter.

Candace took a leave of absence to "find herself." She vacationed in Peru where she met Ricky in a coffee shop. She is now a freedom fighter and listed on the top Most Wanted lists in the country and pregnant with twins.

Janiyah and her family now have dinner with Calvin and his family every Sunday night. Occasionally, Martin joins them. The Voice is a regular topic, but a pleasant one. Currently, they are planning a food drive for the homeless shelter. They already have plenty of baby formula.

56

"I am getting tired of this," Ben tried to yell, but had to keep his voice down. This was their second trip to the airport bathroom and already he felt uneasy about it. He thought that two young, goofy-looking janitors would stand out, especially two standing together in the men's bathroom, arguing.

"Come on, one last time."

"Then we are done?"

"Then we are done."

They spoke easier now that the last person had left the bathroom. No other flights were due in for over an hour so they had plenty of free time to work. Jerry looked through their equipment, pulling each part out one by one. It was then that Jerry remembered the microphone.

"Did you get the new batteries?"

"No, I thought you did."

Jerry turned the microphone upside down and opened up the battery compartment. Inside was empty. He shook the microphone again, hoping that somehow a battery hiding inside would drop out, there was nothing there. With an expression of disbelief he turned to Ben.

"When did you last check the microphone?"

"Never, that was your job. When did you last check it?"

"Maybe a month ago when I took the old batteries out and asked you to put new ones in. I thought maybe you put the old ones back in until you got new ones."

"But that was your job, so I stayed out of it."

Ben peered into the bottom of the microphone to see what Jerry was getting so upset about. What he saw did not make sense.

"Where are the batteries?"

Jerry turned his stare from the microphone and back to Ben. He had no answer and hoped Ben did. Ben had no answer, either. For a moment the two just stood in the restroom, wondering what this meant. Then a voice echoed across the room.

"Ben, Jerry, this is God. I need you to save my people."

Printed in the United States
By Bookmasters